Beachside Bliss

Beachside Bliss

A sweet vacation romance

Kasey Kennedy

Beachside Bliss

Seaside Bay, Book 2

Copyright © 2025 by Kasey Kennedy

All rights reserved.

No part of this publication may be reproduced, stored in a retrieval system, or transmitted in any form or by any means, electronic, mechanical, photocopying, recording, scanning, or otherwise, without the prior written permission except in brief quotations in a book review.

This is a work of fiction. All characters, organizations, and events portrayed in this novel are either products of the author's imagination or are used fictitiously. Any resemblance to persons, living or dead, incidents, and places is coincidental. This is a work of personal creation; no Artificial Intelligence was used in the creation of this manuscript.

ISBN-13: 978-1-958942-18-5 (paperback)

ISBN-13: 978-1-958942-17-8 (e-book)

Cover design by Deborah Bradseth

Author Website:

www.kasey-kennedy.com

Published by:

White Eagle Rock Publishing

Other Books by Kasey Kennedy:

IN BLOOM SERIES:
Peonies for Paige
Dahlias for Dominica
Lilies for Lauren
Tulips for Tilly
Wildflowers for Anna Lee

MISTLETOE KISSES SERIES:
Mistletoe for Tricia

SEASIDE BAY SERIES:
Poolside Promises
Beachside Bliss

Other Books:
Love and Pumpkins
Love and Lights
Happy Holidates

To Karen Wolfram-Istok,
Memories of our vacations together make me smile!
I'm thankful we've reconnected!

Chapter 1

"I'm going to miss you," Sorcha Pedigo whispered as she stared at the sparkling Gulf of Mexico, remembering the fantastic day spent floating in the water with her best friend Linda, laughing and working on their tans.

To counteract the pushing and pulling from the waves, they had found a concrete block and tied it to their floats with a long, heavy-duty rope. They walked ten yards into the water, dropped the block and wedged it into the sand to keep them bobbing on the waves and not floating into shore. It had taken several attempts to jump up on the floats at that depth, which only added to their merriment.

The light from the setting sun rippled over the waves, and the sky dazzled with broad strokes of pinks and purples wafting across the horizon. She imagined sharing a picture of the view with her students and having them paint it as an art project.

Taking a deep breath of the briny gulf air, she closed her eyes to capture the sensation of being here in Seaside Bay, Florida. Tomorrow, she and Linda would fly home. On Monday, she'd be back in her classroom full of rambunctious third graders, who, having tasted the freedom of spring break, would start their countdowns to summer vacation.

They wouldn't be alone in that countdown to freedom.

After eight years of teaching math, reading, and science to her students, Sorcha was ready for something new.

It wasn't just the years of teaching that caused her angst. She would turn thirty in May and having spent her spring break with her roommate planning Linda's wedding, the march of age seemed to propel her towards a great unknown.

She loved teaching. She loved the kids. But the prospect of thirty-five years (or more!) of it was overwhelming her.

There had to be more to life than earning a paycheck and hanging out with friends. Yes, she was teaching and nurturing children, and that was fulfilling, but she wanted even more out of life.

She glanced at her phone to check the time. She needed to go inside and get ready for their last night on the town. Well, as much "on the town" as quaint little Seaside Bay, whose population consisted primarily of retirees and beach bums, could provide.

Back in the condo, Sorcha smiled to hear the stereo blasting "All the Single Ladies". It had been their "go-to" song all week. Linda's days as a single lady were numbered. She would marry in July, leaving Sorcha one of the last single ladies in their peer group.

Sorcha didn't mind being the last woman standing; she had promised herself she would not settle for Mr. Alright, spoken with a shrug. She wanted Mr. Right. A man who saw her for who she was deep inside, not for her outward appearance. She'd dated too many men who were happy to have her hanging off their arm, as long as she kept smiling and was agreeable. As soon as she spoke her mind or rallied for the oppressed, or spoke out against injustice, they ran.

Good riddance. Don't let the door hit ya.

Linda popped her head out of the bathroom, hearing the front door shut behind Sorcha. "Oh, you're back! Yay!"

"In the flesh." Sorcha pasted on a smile and joined her friend in the bathroom. "What are you doing?" she asked, spying the assortment of hair accessories strewn about the counter.

"Trying to decide how to wear my hair. I think it looks good down, but after twenty minutes outside in the wind and humidity, my hair will resemble Medusa's snarly locks."

"Tell me about it," Sorcha said, rolling her eyes. Though her straight blond tresses rarely frizzed with humidity, the thin, shoulder-length cut was susceptible to wind-blown tangles.

Sorcha picked up a claw clip that Linda favored. "What if I do a pretty twist and clip your hair in this, leaving a few of your purple strands loose around your face?"

"Yes! Please!" Linda enthusiastically replied.

They chatted about outfit choices and dinner options. Linda wanted to drive to a restaurant forty minutes away, but Sorcha argued. "No driving! We're going to hit it hard tonight!" Linda laughed and gave in.

Dinner was casual. The roommates talked about their careers and futures. Sorcha felt like she still had more questions than answers about her own future. Not knowing how transferable her teaching degree would be was challenging. She was interested in pursuing a corporate training role, but wasn't sure which industries to consider. She didn't want to work for a large conglomerate. The thing she loved best about teaching was the small community of teachers, aides, and administrators. She was a name, not a number.

There were several large insurance companies and hospitals in her community. She disliked either choice. Insurance was too numbers-focused, and she couldn't stand to be in a hospital since her mom had died.

When her stepbrother Jacob's Achilles tendon ruptured during a soccer match, her dad had chastised her for refusing to go to the emergency room with them. She'd walked four miles home and waited hours for them to return.

That had only been two years after her mom died, but even now, ten years later, she couldn't stand the thought of entering a hospital. When her doctor's practice moved into the fifth floor of the newly constructed hospital, she found another doctor in a tiny office for her annual checkups.

After dinner, the women strolled to Crabbie's, a dive bar close to Linda's family's condo, where they were staying. With an anything-goes vibe, cheap drinks, and live music loud enough to keep the over-sixty crowd at bay, it was their favorite local bar.

Sorcha spied two open seats at the bar and tilted her head for Linda to follow. She squeezed past a group of dude bros, ignoring their raucous chatter. She was not in the mood for some drunk to hit on her tonight.

Settling in at the bar, she frowned to see Jasmyn behind the bar. "Where's Q?" she asked when Jasmyn came over to get their drink orders.

"He asked for a night off," Jasmyn said, in her dry voice. She raised a pierced eyebrow at them. "He must have known you were coming in."

"Hey, now," Sorcha replied. "Quincy loves me."

Jasmyn laughed as she popped the top of the beer bottle Sorcha had requested. "Quincy doesn't love another living soul."

"Ha, ha. He'll eventually fall for me. It's just a matter of time."

"Yeah, we'll see." Jasmyn set Sorcha's beer and Linda's cocktail on the bar and walked away.

Linda twirled the swizzle stick with the pink crab topper and sighed. "I know you think Quincy is hot, but I think you just like him because he's unattainable."

"Unattainable? How do you figure?"

"He lives in Florida; you live in Illinois. You like the thrill of the chase, and he's covered with 'stay back' caution signs."

"Caution signs?"

"Yeah. Those dark tattoos."

Sorcha shrugged. "I love his tattoos. Besides, long-distance love affairs work. Look at you and Mason."

"Once we found each other again, we were only long-distance for a few months before he moved back home. Quincy doesn't seem like the relocation type. And you've never talked about moving. You seem to be settled in Bloomington. You have your school there; your dad is there. It's home."

Sorcha nodded but refrained from saying anything. She knew Bloomington was H.O.M.E. for Linda, but she told herself it would be easy to move. Maybe not *easy*, but doable.

Yes, she appreciated being physically close to her dad, and she loved the apartment she shared with Linda, but their days together were dwindling. Once Linda married Mason in July, they planned to live in Mason's apartment while saving for a down payment on a house.

Sorcha wasn't sure what that meant for her own living arrangements. The lease was up at the end of August, but that wasn't an ideal time to move. School would start again in mid-August, and she had no desire to move over the three-day Labor Day weekend.

Besides, it would be hard to afford the rent on her own. She hated staring at spreadsheets, trying to make a budget, which would inevitably fail days later when she found a shirt or pair of jeans on sale. *Hello? Sale!* Sometimes you have to spend money to save money.

But she knew even the simplest math didn't work. Her monthly salary, minus the rent on her own, was no good. She missed her college days, when she'd pay a year's rent with each new student loan. It was too cringe-inducing to consider that, since she was still paying off her loans, she was still paying for college rent years after she'd moved out. So she didn't think about it.

"I'm not sure about settling." Sorcha swished her bottle before taking a sip. "I need to find a new place to live.

Maybe I should sell all my furniture and move in with my dad."

"Are you sure about that? Didn't you say you couldn't stand his wife?"

"I'm supposed to say that. She's honestly a good stepmom. I shouldn't complain."

"Could you really live at home again?"

Sorcha sighed. "No, I don't want to. Especially with my stepbrothers still at home. But maybe this is my opportunity to set new goals. Change directions."

"That's the looming birthday talking." Linda shook her head, and a few strands of her hair came out of the clip. "Besides, you don't want to give your dad the satisfaction of saying, "I told you so," if you tell him that you can't afford to live on your own. I know you."

Sorcha tried to pretend her upcoming milestone birthday wasn't bothering her, but since her best friend had gotten engaged, it weighed on her mind more and more.

"You're right. Do you think it's just the birthday blues? I wouldn't know. I've never turned thirty before." She smiled at Linda. "Hey, this is our last night here in sunny Seaside Bay before you get married. No more talk about birthdays, apartments, or bills. Let's kick things up a notch."

A gentleman twice their age sat on the empty stool on the other side of Linda. He had a dark tan, gray hair at his temples, and an expensive watch. Sorcha leaned her head over the bar to get a better look at him.

"Hey there!" she called.

"Hello." He turned towards them with a smile, a twinkle in his eye, and a charming gap in his front teeth. "How are you ladies this evening?"

"Better now that you're here. I'm Sorcha. And this is my best friend, Linda. She's engaged, so no hitting on her."

The man chuckled and held out his hand to Linda. "Hello, Linda. I'm Michael."

"Pleased to meet you," Linda replied. "Don't mind Sorcha. She's a mostly harmless flirt."

Sorcha reached over to shake his hand. "Mostly is questionable. Do you live in Seaside Bay, Michael?"

"I live just a couple of blocks away. At the Mockingbird."

"Oh, really?" Linda pushed her empty drink glass towards Jasmyn, who was checking on them. "My family has a condo there. That's where we're staying."

"But we're leaving tomorrow," Sorcha added. "Don't get any ideas. No wedding ring?"

"I took it off to golf today. Forgot to put it back on."

"Oh," Sorcha said, her eyes narrowing, with an enormous grin stretching across her face. This was fun. "Really?"

"Don't get your hackles up. My husband will be here shortly."

"Ah, great! Do you dance, Michael?"

"Like Madonna's backup dancer."

Oh, this will be fun! A chance to let go, dance, and not worry about getting hit on. "Let's go!" Sorcha said, hopping off her stool. "Hold the fort, Linda Lu."

"Always. Shake it, girlie."

Chapter 2

Quincy listened to the voicemail for the fourth time. Yes, he was Quincy Halford. Yes, he'd lived in Myrtle Beach two years ago. And yes, he knew Leeza Shelton.

But no.

There was absolutely no way he'd fathered a child.

Leeza would have told him. She would have held it over his head and demanded child support. When he'd broken up with her, she'd barely protested. But that might have been because she was high on something.

He should have seen the signs sooner. He'd been around enough users in his life to be wary of newcomers who liked to have a good time all the time.

Shaking his head, he shook off the memories of Myrtle Beach and Leeza.

This must be a mistake. He grabbed the electric bill envelope and flipped it over to jot down notes. Today's date, May twenty-ninth, caller name, phone number, and something about a kid.

Getting the info on a piece of paper calmed his nerves. Seeing the words written out made them manageable. He could react to the words. He would return the phone call, speak to Ms. Myer, and clear up this misunderstanding.

Heaven forbid! If by some chance he had a kid, he would find out how to make child-support payments, and then he'd move on. He'd done a fine job ruining his own life. He wouldn't risk ruining a kid's.

He wouldn't even tell his mother or sister about this incident.

Before making the call, he grabbed the bottle of Jack Daniels from the counter. He would need a drink either to celebrate the colossal mistake or to drown his regrets if this was true and he had a child with Leeza. Hitting REDIAL on his phone, he put the glass down and picked up the pen, ready to take more notes if needed.

"Hello?" This was obviously the same person who had left the voice mail. Her drawl reminded him of lazy Sundays and key lime pie.

"Yes. This is Quincy Halford. You left a message for me regarding Leeza Shelton."

"Oh, right, Mr. Halford. Thanks for calling me back so quickly. We are definitely under a time crunch here."

"You said something about a child?"

"Yes, I have terrible news. Ms. Shelton passed away a few weeks back."

"Overdose?"

The woman sighed softly. "I'm not at liberty to say. But you can request a coroner's report yourself. Next of kin and all."

"I'm not next of kin. We weren't married."

"Well, I understand. But there is no other family, and you were identified as the child's father."

"By whom?" Quincy rubbed his head.

"By Leeza. She named you as the father on the birth certificate. I verified with several of Leeza's friends that you two were together at the right time."

"That proves nothing. She could have been messing around even while we dated."

"It's possible. And you can request a DNA test to confirm paternity. But the issue at hand concerns custody. The longer the child is in the foster care system—"

Quincy cut her off. "Leeza had a mother."

"Unfortunately, she's passed as well."

"I can't help you." Quincy shook his head, even though the woman on the other end of the line couldn't see him. "I don't have the means to take care of a child, even if it is mine. I can help with financial support but that's all I can do."

"No, that won't help. If she stays in the system..."

"She?"

"Yes," the woman laughed. "Sorry. I didn't mention that. Yes, she. Eva Lyn, she's a precocious little thing with the brightest blue eyes."

Quincy glanced up from the envelope where he'd just written "Eva Lyn". That was his grandma's name. He'd told Leeza how special his grandparents had been to him growing up. Had she named her daughter after his grandmother? Was that somehow supposed to convince him the baby was his?

"Eva Lyn?"

"Yes; you really need to see your daughter, Mr. Halford."

"You seem pretty convinced she's mine."

"I am."

"How old is she?"

"Ah, you're trying to do the math. She's almost eighteen months."

That was in the ballpark.

"I'm telling you—" Quincy took a breath to steady himself. He didn't want to shout. "There is no way I can take care of a kid. It's just me, and I work full time."

Kid. He couldn't call her by that name. Couldn't think about bright blue eyes and family names. He just couldn't.

"We can always find a way," Quincy heard the bristle in Ms. Myer's voice. "Just because you haven't done something before doesn't mean you can't in the future."

Was this woman certified in motivational speeches?

He shook his head, even though she couldn't see him. "You can't just spring this on a person."

"I know it's a surprise. Take some time to digest it. It'll take me a week or so to get everything together. A judge will need to grant temporary custody, and I'll need to make travel arrangements. I'll call you again in the morning. We have a lot to discuss. In the meantime, I'll send a list of baby items you'll need, including Eva Lyn's sizes. She's rather petite for her age. We'll talk soon, Mr. Halford."

She hung up, and Quincy stood grasping the phone for several seconds before he thought of putting it down. He grabbed the tumbler of brown liquid and downed it in a gulp.

This can't be real. It's not happening. Am I dreaming? There's no way. No way. A daughter?

He leaned back in his chair, his eyes tracing a long crack in the ceiling. One more issue with this house to add to the long list of issues. This wasn't a home for a child. It was bachelor-worthy at best.

There was no yard. The Florida heat caused vines and shrubs to take hold everywhere. There was only one bedroom, his. He couldn't put a crib in the living room.

His mind shuffled through options. He would have to move, perhaps live closer to his sister. His mom might be an option, as she'd retire soon, but he had no desire to go back to New Jersey, back to the awful memories and the possibility of running into his ex-wife.

But if he moved, according to his original plan, farther west, how would he manage with a child? How would he even travel with a kid? He would have to rent something and haul his motorcycle.

With more questions than answers, he poured himself another glass of whiskey, larger than the first one, and gulped it down.

He'd probably wake up with a headache and an even worse attitude, but maybe the alcohol would dull the trepidation and pain, for the evening at least.

The next morning, with a hangover and an even worse mood, Quincy dressed quickly and jumped on his motorcycle. He'd become claustrophobic in the small house and needed to escape.

The news about his daughter was just the cherry on top of his hectic and stressful week.

His mother had called on Tuesday to ask for a loan until her next paycheck arrived, because her car needed new spark plugs.

His sister Lainey had called Wednesday, asking if he was ever going to make a firm plan for visiting this summer. He wanted to visit, but with her family's busy schedule, he had to plan a visit weeks in advance, and he preferred more spur-of-the-moment plans.

The landlord had said he needed to schedule roofers to replace the shingles damaged during the last hurricane, and as if that wasn't bad enough, he said he had to raise the rent by forty percent if Quincy signed another lease.

And then the call from Ms. Myer telling him about Eva Lyn.

No wonder he'd fallen into the whiskey bottle.

Now, after a forty-minute drive, he pulled into the public parking lot at Boca Beach.

Hoping there were no rug-rats running around causing havoc and destruction, Quincy Halford removed his helmet and set it on the seat of his motorcycle. His eyes scanned the beach's parking lot. Thankfully, there were few minivans, so hopefully, fewer kids.

Not that he would be beachside for long. He wasn't the type to play in the surf or lie in the sunshine, not having the patience for those activities. He was just here to breathe the fresh, tingly air of the Gulf.

The ten-hour shifts he'd worked for the last eight days and the steady stream of late nights, drunken jerks, and far too many come-ons from women aged twenty-one to ninety-one had his skin crawling and his nerves shot.

He moved to a bench to remove his boots and socks. While he was there, he might as well take a walk. He secured his belongings on the bike and stepped onto the soft, white sand. The tension behind his neck seemed to race down his back and into the sand itself. He imagined fulgurites forming beneath each step, his tension as fiery hot as a lightning strike.

Ignoring the shouts of a couple of teenagers tossing a Frisbee, he made his way closer to the water and the hard-packed sand.

When a feisty wave of water hit his feet, he paused, the cool water jolting his system. Closing his eyes, he took a deep breath and tried to squelch the racket of thoughts shouting for attention in his weary mind.

Yes, Quincy enjoyed living in Seaside Bay, with its proximity to beaches like this. It was home number two after leaving the Northeast. He'd decided New Jersey was no longer for him after his stunning divorce four years ago.

Since leaving, he'd spent two years in Myrtle Beach and the last two years here. Since his lease would be up in September, he needed to decide where to go next. Before the news about his daughter, it'd been a toss-up between New Orleans or Galveston. He wanted to loop the United States, eventually stopping near Seattle. He never wanted to return to the Northeast and risk running into his ex-wife.

The one thing his marriage had taught him was that he didn't belong in a relationship. It was too much pressure, too much compromise.

He was a loner. He didn't want to be tied down to a place, a person, a lifestyle, or a career.

Tending bar was fine for now. It was keeping the bills paid with a little extra to send to his mom now and then. The additional financial responsibility and time commitments that came with caring for a child would require him to think about other career choices.

A few more deep breaths and the mind-noise stilled. With quieter thoughts and a long drive home, maybe he could figure out what he was going to do about Eva Lyn.

Back at his motorcycle, he pulled his phone out of a saddlebag and checked it for any messages. None. Just the way he liked it. No fresh crisis to handle. No new cry for help from his mom or sister. And no further contact from Ms. Myer.

A large van pulled into the space next to his, and a frazzled mom climbed out of the front seat and began unloading kids and a wagon with large, beach-appropriate wheels, which she began loading with tote bags and a cooler.

"Need help?" Quincy called out, standing next to his bike.

"Um, no. I think we got this," the woman replied, warily looking him over.

Quincy chuckled under his breath. He knew he looked intimidating. "Suit yourself," he replied, mounting the bike. He turned the key in the ignition and laughed at the look of horror which passed over the woman's face as he walked the bike back out of the parking spot.

Within minutes, he was back on the road and reaching cruising speed. The rumble of the bike's engine released the tension in his neck caused by the brief chat with the minivan-driving woman.

He knew his outward appearance—the beard, the dark clothing, dusty black boots, and the tattoos crawling up both arms and onto his neck—caused strangers to pause and back off. That was by design. It made it easier to keep people at arm's-length. He lacked the capacity for relationships, romantic or otherwise.

His sister and mom put up with him because they had to. They were family. Besides, he usually came through when they needed him. Usually. That hadn't always been the case. For years, he'd partied hard, worrying only about the next drink. It hadn't bothered him then. He'd seen his dad do the same and assumed there was no other path available to him.

His childhood memories were mostly painful. His dad couldn't keep a job, which caused stress and chaos at home. The fights between his parents were hours-long shouting matches peppered with flying objects and phone calls to the police.

The only real reprieve had been when his grandfather took him camping in the Catskill Mountains.

Quincy loved it when his grandpa picked him up from school on Friday nights and took the three-and-a-half-hour drive to their favorite campsite in the mountains. They would talk about school while listening to a New York Yankees game on the radio. Grandpa never asked Quincy about his home life, though he would ask if there was anything Quincy wanted to talk about. Quincy usually muttered a simple "no".

Camping with Granddad was the only balm that soothed his sore heart. Being outdoors, with only the sounds of nature, the birds, the wind, the streams where they fished, was priceless to the city boy who would feel sick to his stomach when he heard police and ambulance sirens.

Quincy wished his grandpa was still around. But the men in his family died young: his mom's dad at sixty-two, his dad's dad at fifty-one, and his own dad at forty-nine. His dad didn't die from natural causes, though, no stroke or heart attack. He'd done someone wrong one too many times and paid the ultimate price on the wrong side of a pistol.

The way Quincy looked at it, at forty-three, he was an old man. He probably had about a decade left. He was thankful he had little to put in order. No property, no investments, no precious collections to disperse.

If things had continued this way, he'd happily die not owing anyone anything, leaving a few hundred dollars in the bank that his sister could claim. She could take her family out to a nice dinner and maybe raise a toast to good ol' Uncle Q.

That had sounded pretty good to Quincy.

Until now. Now that he had a daughter, he'd have to plan and prepare for her care if something happened to him.

Pulling up in front of his small, rented home, Quincy shut off the engine and walked up the three steps to his tiny porch, glancing around for the stray cats and dog that he fed. If it weren't for a smattering of mangrove trees, shrubs, and dune grasses, he'd have a view of the gulf from this vantage point. The house faced west, and occasionally he took a walk through the grove to sit on the beach and watch the sunset.

At least he could hear the wind blowing through the branches and waves hitting the beach thirty yards away. Whenever a storm blew in, he'd sit on the porch to watch lightning split the sky and listen to nature's wrath. The ferocity would typically match his own mood.

No such luck today. The light breeze barely moved the gardenia bushes in front of his house. He'd have to settle for music to drown out his troubled thoughts.

At least he was far enough away from any other houses not to hear the domestic chatter of young families playing or couples fighting. This small house with no on-site laundry or central air was both cheap enough and private enough to suit Quincy's taste. He could crank some Soundgarden and not worry about a neighbor calling the police.

Music, with pen and paper to figure out what to do about Eva Lyn.

Chapter 3

Sorcha skimmed the wine list. She didn't really want wine, but her dad, Dean, had made reservations at this fancy restaurant to celebrate her thirtieth birthday, so she might as well.

Barb, her stepmom, couldn't make it, which meant her stepbrothers weren't there, and Sorcha got the impression her dad wanted her all to himself.

Shocking, as it mostly felt like her dad preferred the company of his new family to Sorcha's. He got along so well with Aiden and Jacob, his stepsons, that new people they met never suspected that Dean was their stepfather. Meanwhile, Sorcha felt like an outsider in her own family.

Sometimes Sorcha wondered if it was because she'd been so close to her mom. Had Dean felt shut out of the mother-daughter dynamic? He had loved Carrie completely. Sorcha knew that. Carrie's death, from an aggressive lung cancer that was discovered too late, had devastated him as much as it had Sorcha. It'd come completely out of the blue. Carrie had a lingering cough but had chalked it up to seasonal allergies, then laughed as she said she was allergic to something every season.

Losing her mom had changed the trajectory of Sorcha's life. One of the first things she'd done after her mom's funeral was to change her college major.

Sorcha had no longer felt she had the stamina to go to grad school and get the art history degree she'd longed for up to that point. For weeks, it was all she could do just to get out of bed.

"Have you decided?" Dean asked.

Sorcha glanced up from the swimming words on the page. "Sorry?"

"Wine. Did you decide on wine?"

She sighed and put the menu down. "I'll have a glass of the house cab."

Dean looked at the server. "Make that two."

Browsing dinner selections, Dean asked Sorcha how her work was going.

"Same as always." She shrugged. "Kids are rowdy. They want to play, not learn. I'll be glad when school's out."

Dean chuckled. "You've been saying that for twenty-five years."

Sorcha laughed. "I guess you're right. What can you do?"

She perused the menu and decided on a filet mignon. If Dad was picking up the tab, she'd eat well.

"How's the family?" Sorcha asked. "Why couldn't Barb make it?"

"She had a hair appointment." Dean closed his menu and leaned forward. "She couldn't change it. She wanted to, but I told her it was fine. I wanted you all to myself tonight."

Sorcha nodded. It was nice having her dad to herself for a change. "Well, tell her hello for me. And the boys?"

"Both had to work tonight."

The server arrived and placed their glasses of wine on the table. Dean raised his glass towards the center of the table. "A toast to my baby girl. Happy thirtieth, sweetheart."

"Thanks, Dad." Sorcha smiled, a feeling of contentment settling over her. Being thirty wasn't so bad when you were still someone's baby girl.

"There's something important that I need to share with you." Dean set his glass down and folded his hands on the table.

Uh oh. I don't like the sound of this. I don't want bad news tonight. Sorcha slowly set her glass down as well, thankful her hand hadn't shaken, giving away her apprehension.

"When your mother died, there was a small life insurance policy. I took that money and put it in a sort of trust fund for you."

"A sort of trust fund?"

"Well, how about an unofficial trust? An investment account with you named as the beneficiary if anything happened to me. Now that you're thirty, I think it's time to turn over the reins to you with one small stipulation."

Sorcha shook her head. "You want me to manage an investment account? Dad, I struggle with my checking account."

Dean's lips twitched, and his nose crinkled. "I've gotten that impression. That leads to the stipulation. You can leave the money alone and keep it invested, your rainy-day fund. Or you can withdraw it. Now, here's the stipulation: half of the money must be used to purchase a home. The rest you can use to get out of debt…"

He paused and raised an eyebrow, as if to ask if she had any debt. Sorcha shrugged her shoulders as if to say, "Of course, I have debt."

He continued, "Or purchase needed things—maybe you could upgrade that car of yours."

Sorcha disliked the ten-year-old Camry she had bought from a guy who lived in their building when her last car broke down, but it got her around town.

If there's money for a car and a down payment, how much is there?

She blinked at him. It was like his words weren't computing. If there had been a life insurance policy, why couldn't that have been used to pay for her college? Could she have graduated from school debt-free? Could she have paid for graduate school? Not that she had the brainpower for grad school then, but maybe...

When she said nothing for several seconds, Dean leaned forward. "Sweetheart?"

Was there enough money that she could seriously consider changing careers? Get an apartment without a roommate? She shivered at the idea of living alone, but at least it might be financially possible.

She swallowed, her throat feeling like it had forgotten how to move moisture away from her mouth. "How much?" she said, with a shaky voice and a shallow breath.

"Did I forget that part?"

"Yes."

He chuckled. "Sorry. It's around a hundred thousand. So, not a lot. You won't be able to purchase a home with it, but half would make a very nice down payment on a small family home."

Is he trying to dig a knife in? I don't have a family.

"A hundred thousand dollars? Like a one and five zeros?"

She could picture herself writing that large number on the chalkboard, her students ooh-ing and ah-ing.

"Yes, a one and five zeros." He nodded. "It'll help you out, right?"

"Um, yeah." She exaggerated the sound of the words. "Of course. I'm still paying for my college loans, Dad. I could have used that money to pay for college. Why did you hold it back?"

"Character building. I thought you would appreciate your education more if you were financially responsible." He glanced down at the salad plate that had been placed in front of him while he wasn't looking. Sorcha noticed her own at the same time.

She ignored the food. "I don't know how I stayed in college after Mom died. It was crushing. But maybe, weirdly, having the student loans helped. They motivated me to keep going. There was no way I was going to quit college, still pay for classes because of the loans, and not end up with a degree. I had to get the degree. It drove me to keep going."

On the surface, her dad's revelation seemed like good news. She could pay off her college loans with part of the money, catch up on bills, and have a good chunk of change for a down payment. But a down payment on a house where? And would a home mortgage just tie her down to a job she no longer loved?

And why would she go out and buy a house while she was still single?

"I don't think I'm in a position to buy a house right now. I..." She paused. If she told her dad that she was thinking about a career change, would he support her or see it as just another one of her "flighty ideas"? Buying a house would show responsibility, right? Isn't that what she wanted? To be seen as a responsible adult in her dad's eyes?

Shouldn't he want her to be happy?

Dean was halfway through his salad. Sorcha still couldn't find the right words to express what she was feeling.

"What do I need to do?" she finally asked.

"Do?" He smiled as he looked up at her, his light blue eyes just a shade lighter than hers.

"How do I get access to the money? I would like to pay off my student loans as quickly as possible."

"That's a great idea! What about a house? There is a new subdivision being built near us. Small starter homes. Perfect for a single woman."

Starter homes for single women. Sounds absolutely ridiculous. "I'm under lease in the apartment until late August. Linda will move out after her wedding in July. I was thinking about finding someone else to live with me. I love the apartment."

"Find another roommate? Hey, maybe Aiden would like to move in with you. You're close to the college campus.

He was planning to live at home and commute, but maybe he'd like to get out on his own."

"Well, he wouldn't be on his own. He'd be with me. His stepsister." Sorcha shuddered. "After working with third graders all day, I'm not going home to babysit Aiden."

"It wouldn't be babysitting..."

"My answer is no."

"All right, just a thought. You're thirty years old. It's a good time to buy a house."

"That's not a priority for me right now. I like to think I'll get married someday and find a house with my husband. Sure, I could do it on my own, don't get me wrong, but I don't want to. Besides—" she cut herself off.

"Besides?"

She let out a sigh. Better to plow forward. When else would she get the chance to have this one-on-one conversation with her dad? "I'm thinking about a possible career change."

Dean seemed to brace himself, but at least he wasn't protesting. "Oh?"

"I enjoy teaching, but I feel like it's time for something else. Maybe I could find a job working with adults, something more financially rewarding, where I could use my creativity."

"Won't you miss your summers off and two-week break at Christmas?"

"Yes, I will, but vacations aren't the full picture. I am ready for something else."

"When did this come up?"

"What do you mean?"

"How long have you had this change of heart about teaching?" He looked annoyed.

Surely, he didn't think the idea had just come up when she'd heard about her inheritance!

"Awhile. But I think it started becoming more concrete when Linda got engaged. She's moving on. She's growing up. Maybe it's time I do the same."

"You're thirty. You've been a grownup for years now, Sorcha."

"Maybe. But I don't feel like I've got it all figured out. I'm not mature and successful. I don't know what I want to be when I grow up!"

Their entrees arrived, and the smell of the butter-ladened steak made Sorcha sigh. Or maybe that was the conversation with her dad.

"It's time to figure it out. Though with your shiny object syndrome, I am surprised you haven't changed careers a half dozen times by now."

Ouch. Nothing like getting berated by your dad at your birthday dinner... At least Barb and the boys aren't here to witness it this time. A miracle.

Eight days. In eight days, school will be out, and I'll be on a plane to Florida for much-needed R and R.

Linda had arranged for Sorcha to spend two weeks at her uncle's condo. It would be Sorcha's first time staying there alone, and with all the ideas swimming in her head about what to do with her life, she was looking forward to the time away to plan the next step.

Double blessings. The chance to stay in a beautiful condo on the beach and now a sudden financial windfall. What a lucky girl I am!

Sorcha changed the subject to focus on Aiden and Jacob's summer plans. Her dad could carry an entire conversation on his own when it came to those two young men.

After dinner, they ordered dessert, a slice of cheesecake for Dean and a chocolate lava cake for Sorcha. The server brought out her dessert with a single candle on it, and Dean softly crooned "Happy Birthday" to her. The smile in his eyes and the earnestness in his voice made Sorcha tear up.

He walked her to her car when they left the restaurant. Pointing out some rust on the side panel, he encouraged her to consider upgrading the car. Illinois winters and all the salt on the roads were tough on cars, he'd said.

"I know, Dad. I have a lot to think about."

"You do. Call me if you want to talk anything over, and I'll email you tomorrow with the account information. Remember, half for a house."

"Half for a house," she repeated. She stood on her toes to kiss his cheek. "Night, Dad. Thank you again. The shock is wearing off. I can't tell you how grateful I am that you did this for me. If you'd handed that money over to me when I was in college, I probably would have been reckless with it. I'll do a much better job managing it now. I love you."

He smiled. "I love you, sweetheart. Good night."

Chapter 4

What was I thinking? I should have invited someone to come on this vacation with me! Sure, an empty condo on the beach had sounded good when Linda proposed it, but now that Sorcha was here, she was miserable.

And it was only day three of fourteen. How was she going to survive eleven more days alone?

Her goal for this trip was to come up with her next career move. With her dad's news about the nest egg, she felt even more determined to figure it out.

But it wasn't enough money to pay off student loans *and* pay for graduate school, so she wasn't sure how beneficial it could be.

She strolled down La Playa Parkway towards Crabbie's, nodding to the few passersby and window-shopping at the handful of shops along the way. It was a gorgeous evening, and people were out enjoying the cooler evening after the day's blistering heat.

She was hoping there would be several patrons in the bar so she could have a proper conversation with someone, anyone, but on a Monday night, she wasn't sure that the odds would be in her favor.

Stepping into the small bar, she scanned the room. Being a weeknight, the atmosphere was more laid back, and the music was at a low volume, so it was easy to carry on a conversation. A couple at a high-top table near the open wall were having a heated argument, and two older women perched on bar stools. She knew who she wanted to talk to, and hopefully he'd be behind the bar tonight, so she asked the women at the bar if they minded some company.

"No, sugar. Pull up a seat," the closest one said.

The woman sported painted-on purple eyebrows and glitter eyeshadow. Impressive. The purple reminded her of Linda's current hair color. She'd have to tell her roommate about the purple eyebrows.

"I'm Sorcha. Can I buy the next round?"

"Yes, hon," said the second woman. "I'm Rosalie. That's Winnie."

"Nice to meet you, ladies." She scanned the room. "Where's the bartender?"

"That hunky man went to the back for beers."

Hunky man? Sorcha hoped that meant Quincy, the guy she'd drooled over the last time she'd been in Seaside Bay.

"Quincy?"

"Yes'm. That's the one," Winnie responded, tilting her head back to empty the tall, slender glass in her hand.

The door to the back room swung open, and Sorcha suppressed a gasp. It was definitely Quincy, and he looked hotter than ever.

He wore a tight-fitting dark gray T-shirt, black jeans, and black boots. A short black apron was slung low around his waist. Sorcha noticed that his hair was a little longer than the last time she'd seen him, not shaggy, just longer. His beard was about the same length, not long, but long enough to imagine getting her fingers in it. She noticed there were a few more gray hairs on top of his head and in his beard.

He carried a case of beer bottles on his shoulder; his tattoo-covered arm flexed in body builder bicep perfection.

Sorcha didn't miss the wink when he saw her. The gesture caused her stomach to flip-flop.

He set the case on the counter and walked towards her. "Win and Rose, I see you gained a companion. Careful, she's trouble."

"Trouble, you say. I think she's adorable, Quincy!" Winnie said, pushing her empty glass towards him. "And she's got the next round. Make mine a double."

"Yes, ma'am. Rose?"

"Same. A double." Rosalie set her empty glass down with a thud. Sorcha wondered how many drinks the ladies had consumed and if they had far to go to get home.

"And what about you, money bags?" Quincy put his hands on his hips and Sorcha licked her lips.

"A mojito, please. Make mine a double, too."

Quincy shook his head and grabbed three clean glasses from the shelf.

"Where you from, hon?" Rosalie tilted her head, her blond bob brushing the top of her blouse, a red one with sparkly gemstones scattered over the shoulders.

"Bloomington, Illinois." Sorcha flicked her eyes between Rosalie and Quincy frequently. "I'm here on vacation."

"Oh, yeah? Where ya staying?" Winnie asked, leaning forward to see past Rosalie.

"At the Mockingbird."

"Oh, lovely. That's where I live. Winnie is staying with me. She's visiting from Alabama."

"Oh." Sorcha stuck out her lip. "I wish I had a friend staying with me. I'm lonely."

"Well, Sugar, you got us now," Winnie cackled. "Rosalie and I have been friends for seventy years. I reckon our friendship can stand a third wheel."

"Seventy years? Wow! That's amazing."

Quincy set their drinks on the bar. "What's amazing?"

Sorcha wanted to shout, "You!" but she held her tongue.

Rosalie picked up her drink and held it up to clink with Winnie and Sorcha. "These double drinks are amazing!"

"Cheers!" Sorcha clinked.

"To the goddess!" Winnie said.

Sorcha chuckled. These two ladies were #lifegoals. She imagined herself and Linda sitting on these same stools, fifty years in the future. She really hoped Linda would have purple eyebrows then.

"Okay, ladies," Sorcha said when Quincy strolled over to help a new group on the other side of the u-shaped bar. "What do you do for fun around here? I'm running out of ideas."

"We mostly shop," Rosalie said, taking a sip of her drink. "Drive to Clearwater or Tampa. We have a list of all the thrift shops within a sixty-mile drive. We like to shop, but on our fixed incomes, we like to save, even more."

"I can relate. Let me know when you go thrifting, if you don't mind company."

Winnie raised her glass. "You offer to buy the drinks, and we'll take you anywhere, Sug'."

"Good to know! Do you ever hang out at the pool?"

The Mockingbird had a lovely bean-shaped pool. Sorcha rarely saw people in it, but there were usually some people sitting at the surrounding tables.

"Oh, yes." Rosalie looked at Sorcha with smiling eyes. "How else are we going to find a man?"

Sorcha coughed and nearly spit out her drink. "Well, there's that. Are you both single?"

"Widowed," Winnie said.

"Divorced for twenty-five years," Rosalie answered.

"So, we're all single and ready to..."

"Mingle!" Winnie yelled, cutting Sorcha off.

Once they finished their drinks, Winnie said they needed to wander back and pass out. Sorcha exchanged numbers with them and asked them to get in touch the next day when they headed to the pool.

After the women left, Sorcha looked around the bar. The couple that had been arguing when she came in were now squeezed closer together, practically sharing a seat.

Quincy cleared the empty glasses that Winnie and Rosalie had left and asked Sorcha where her friend was. He'd never seen her in the bar without Linda.

"I'm here solo on this trip. Linda reserved the condo for me as a birthday present. I thought it would be great to stay by myself, but I hate it already."

"Too bad."

"I know, right? Lovely beach condo all by my lonesome." She sighed. "I'm not the best company when it's just me."

"Good time to do some soul-searching."

"I've got no time to search for that. But I would like to figure out my next career move."

Quincy smirked. "What do you do now?"

"I teach third grade."

"Yikes." His eyes widened.

Sorcha laughed. That was a frequent reaction from adults who'd missed the calling to be a teacher. "Hey, I like to think they'll keep me young. Well, young with gray hairs."

"There's not a gray hair on your head." Quincy glanced around the bar, making sure no one was looking for a refill.

"Well, my beautician is a magician."

"Nice rhyme."

That's what you get when you read primarily third-grade literature. Time to pick up some novels for adults.

She shook her empty glass. "Could I have another mojito, Quincy?"

"Another double?"

"Better make it a single. I have to walk back to the condo, and I hear this can be a dangerous place."

"Only dangerous because you might get in a tussle with a man and his walker."

"Yeah, *that* guy is a rebel."

Quincy laughed, and she enjoyed seeing the way the lines around his eyes crinkled. Why hadn't she dated an older man yet?

"Speaking of dating..."

"We weren't." His smile turned into a smirk.

"Well, maybe I was thinking about it. Why don't we?"

"Why don't we do what?" He tossed the bar towel over his shoulder and leaned both hands on the bar, easing closer to her face.

This she could get used to.

"Date. Let's go on a date. I told you, I'm pretty bored."

He shook his head. "I don't date patrons."

Sorcha tossed her head back. "Fine. I'll leave and go outside. When you get off work, we can talk. I won't be a patron then."

He raised an eyebrow. "I don't get off until two a.m. Besides. I don't date women in their twenties. Come back when you're older."

"It's your lucky day. I turned thirty..." She paused for dramatic effect. "A week ago."

"Good for you." He wiped down the bar. "Doesn't change my mind. You're going to go back home and meet a nice, respectable man who's going to want to marry you."

"No, I won't."

"You will."

"Hasn't happened yet."

"You haven't been ready yet," he replied. " But now that thirty is your reality, you're gonna be ready, and a nice banker or salesperson with a nine-to-five job and a health-benefits package is going to waltz into your life and snatch you up."

Sorcha rolled her eyes. "Yeah, right?"

"Look, I'm going to be moving on soon. Besides, I'm not the dating type."

"Where ya moving?"

"Don't know. Haven't decided."

"Ah, that's my favorite place."

Another patron waved to Quincy, and he walked away.

There's another reason not to fall in love with the sexy bartender. He's not staying here. Well, maybe that's not a bad thing. Seaside Bay is great to visit, but I don't know if I'd want to live here either. It was a thirty-mile drive to a decent shopping center.

She was at a turning point in life, and following Quincy didn't sound like a bad idea. It might not be a great idea, but wouldn't be the worst she'd ever had. There was that one summer at camp when she thought it would be a good idea to knock down a wasp nest that was hanging behind the girls' cabin. Once that thing hit the ground, it was as if a tornado of angry, buzzing wasps would be the end of her.

She'd taken off running and jumped into the lake, swimming underwater to the floating dock. When she surfaced, she counted three stings on her legs, thankful it hadn't been more.

Quincy returned to Sorcha's corner of the bar. "You're still here?"

"I'm not going anywhere, handsome." *Oops, maybe go easy on the mojitos.* She hiccupped.

"That's it. I'm cutting you off."

"But I'm on vacation..." she whined.

"Don't care. Cut off."

"Fine. Can I have a glass of water?"

He got a clean glass and filled it from the sprayer.

After he put it in front of her, she took a long gulp. "Thanks. Now, where are we moving to, Q?"

"Not happening. You'll be lucky if I serve you again if you keep this up."

"Oh, Quincy. I'm just having some fun."

"I'm not your entertainment."

"Yes, sir."

Not yet, but bantering with him was entertaining. What else was a girl to do on vacation alone and at a crossroads in her life?

Chapter 5

I can't believe it's finally happening! Quincy's taking me on a motorcycle ride. Heck, yeah! Sorcha shimmied across the building's lobby as she slid on her sunglasses.

It had taken three days of perseverance; she'd asked several times but wasn't about to give up.

He'd finally agreed when Sorcha upped the ante and said she would bake him chocolate chip cookies. She didn't have them tonight, unable to imagine how they'd carry them on his motorcycle.

She hoped that after the ride, he'd let his guard down enough to tell her where he lived, and she could drop the cookies off at his house.

She contemplated what kind of home he lived in. Would it be like the typical bachelor pad? Messy, without a lot of furniture? Did he have a roommate? She should have asked.

Exiting the building, she sat on an Adirondack chair on the patio overlooking the Gulf. She wouldn't sit long. She wanted to be standing on the curb when Quincy arrived, but she took a moment to relish the sight of the setting sun.

Watching the swelling and undulating waves slowed her breathing and calmed her mind.

After a final cleansing breath, she stood and walked towards the side of the building to a small but adequate turnabout where the road ended and the beach began, offering a convenient pickup and drop-off location for residents and guests of the Mockingbird.

Sorcha glanced up the road, noting the handful of people walking towards the quaint downtown Seaside Bay area.

If Quincy was up for it after the ride, she was going to suggest walking downtown to get an iced coffee. She didn't think Quincy would want to go to the bar on his night off.

Musing whether Quincy would get fancy sweetened coffee or black, she supposed it would be a plain Jane hot coffee.

An older couple, whom Sorcha had seen around the building but hadn't met, walked towards her, hand in hand.

They stopped and commented on the weather. Sorcha wore jeans, tennis shoes, and a light jacket. She felt sweat beading on her back, but Quincy insisted she cover her skin when going for a ride.

As the couple said good night, Sorcha heard the rumble of a motorcycle and glanced up the street. She couldn't hide the smile that broke across her face as she recognized Quincy on his shiny, rumbling machine.

He made a slow, wide turn and stopped next to her.

"Hey," he said, pulling off his helmet.

"Hi. You're prompt."

Sorcha noticed the beads of sweat on his forehead before Quincy ran a handkerchief over it. He stuffed the material in a pocket as he kicked the stand down and climbed off.

"Did you expect me to be late?"

"I wasn't sure."

"I like to be on time."

"Same. But it doesn't always work out."

"You're on time now." He pulled a helmet out of a storage pocket under the seat and handed it to her.

"I've been counting down the hours until this ride."

He smiled quickly, and Sorcha wanted to melt. *How is this man single? He's so dreamy. His smile is enough to make the darkest days feel manageable.*

"Good," he said. "Have you ridden before?"

"Does a moped around the college campus count?"

"No. It does not. Couple things. Keep your mind on the ride. No jerking to the side to look at something along the road. When we come to a curve, lean like I do. If I lean left, you lean left. Don't lean in the opposite direction. That could cause an accident."

Sorcha nodded as she tried to snap on the helmet. After she fumbled for a moment, Quincy leaned closer and pulled the straps from her hands. "Here."

He quickly snapped on the helmet while Sorcha breathed in the scent of him. He smelled like warm leather and mint. The back of his fingers brushed her neck, sending shivers through her. He frowned slightly, and she wondered if he was annoyed by having to help her, or if he was still angry with himself for giving in. The idea spurred her on to ensure the evening was fun for them both.

The weight of the helmet surprised her as her head snapped back. "Whoa," she whispered, adjusting her stance.

Quincy squinted at her. "OK?"

"Yes. Of course." She held up her small cross-body purse. "Can I put this in the trunk?"

He chuckled and lifted the seat cover again. "I'll climb on first and then you. Your feet go there." He pointed out two short bars.

As he swung his leg over the bike, Sorcha's stomach twisted and spasmed. *Am I really ready for this?*

Quincy looked at her and tilted his head slightly. She stood on the footrest and swung her leg over.

"Hang on to me," Quincy said over his shoulder.

This is what I was looking forward to the most!

She wrapped her arms around him, clutching her wrists together, and engulfing him in a hug, leaning against his back. *Hope I'm not too clingy.*

She felt Quincy's stomach muscles clench as he drew in a quick breath. She loosened her grip slightly. He restarted the engine, and it roared to life. A thrill shot through Sorcha's body, and she knew it wasn't an electrical shock from the bike. It was pure adrenaline.

Quincy revved the handles and pushed the kickstand up.

Driving several blocks through downtown Seaside Bay, Sorcha glanced left and right, taking it in. She was mindful to not swing her head or body wildly.

A few minutes later, they were on the coastal road heading north. As Quincy picked up speed, Sorcha gripped his waist tighter and shifted so her body pressed against his back. She wasn't sure, but thought he took in another hard breath.

Sorcha turned her face toward the setting sun, resting the helmet against Quincy's back. It was easier than having all the wind blowing in her face.

Thirty minutes later, Quincy pulled into a beach-access parking lot. Coming to a stop, he turned his head. "You all right?"

"Yes!" she shouted. She was better than all right.

"I'm going to head back to Seaside Bay. I'm not a fan of driving at night on these roads. Too many accidents."

"All right."

She hid her disappointment. She would love to ride for hours, but Quincy was in charge. If he wasn't comfortable driving after dark, it made sense to head back; the sun would soon be down.

Once Quincy pulled into The Mockingbird's parking lot and slid into an available visitor spot, he waited for her to get off the bike before he did.

Her feet back on the ground, Sorcha felt her legs wobble a little.

"Did you enjoy the ride?"

"I feel like I stepped off a boat," she said, unsnapping the helmet.

"We'll have to work on your bike legs, like sea legs."

Sorcha liked the sound of "we" in that sentence. Maybe this wouldn't be a one-time event, though Quincy had put up such resistance to the idea of them hanging out, even as friends.

"Yes. We will."

Handing the helmet back to Quincy, Sorcha worried that her hair, which was naturally thin and straight, was out of control. Out of control, just like her heart beating wildly, as erratic as her breath. She was sure she looked a mess.

"Want to go for a coffee?" Sorcha didn't want to invite Quincy out for a drink. This was not a date in his mind. But coffee was something friends did.

"Where?"

"The Coastal Drip." She pointed towards the shopping district two blocks away. Even though Quincy must be familiar with the place, it was only a block away from his bar, Crabbie's.

"Sure."

Quincy pulled off his jacket and stuffed it in the secure container under the seat. Sorcha wondered what its official name was; maybe she'd ask.

She pulled her own jacket off and slung it over her arm. If she wasn't worried about Quincy taking off, she'd run it up to the condo so she wouldn't have to carry it, but since he was so reluctant to go out with her, she wouldn't risk giving him an excuse to leave.

"So," she started as they began walking, "How long have you been riding a motorcycle?"

"Since I was sixteen. Couldn't afford a car but I could afford a rundown bike."

"Do you have a car?"

"Nope. I keep my possessions to a minimum. Easier to move."

"You can move with just a motorbike?" Her eyes widened. "Please tell me you have a little sidecar that you load up with all your clothes and personal stuff."

"No sidecar. I get where I'm going with a large backpack and a duffel I can strap onto the seat. My saddlebags get loaded. There is no wasted space."

"Wait. You move with two bags and your little containers filled? That's it? Do you own pots and pans?"

"I rent places that are fully furnished. If I find I've accumulated too much stuff when it's time to move on, I take all the extra stuff to a shelter or veteran's center and take just what I need."

"So, no pots and pans."

He shook his head. "Not a one."

"No books, no pictures, no mementos?"

"No, ma'am."

How strange. I know I have too much stuff, but I can't imagine moving to a new place with just a few bags. She could learn a few things from Quincy about being satisfied with enough. "Wow. I can't imagine. Maybe it's easier for men, though. I mean, women have all this jewelry and makeup and a hundred and fifty-seven pairs of shorts. And..."

"That's a lot of shorts."

"Maybe I've exaggerated."

"I hope so."

They reached Coconut Cove Street and had to wait for a couple of cars to pass before continuing. A light breeze blew and whipped Sorcha's hair across her shoulders. She was wearing a tank top, and the hair tickled her neck.

"I think I need to move later this summer, and I dread packing already."

"You *think* you need to move?"

"My roommate Linda is getting married. She'll move out, and I don't think I can afford our apartment on my own."

"Sounds like you need to move."

"Maybe I can find another roommate..." She'd never find a roommate as wonderful as Linda.

"If you move, you could downsize beforehand. It'll save you grief and money."

Sorcha shook her head. "I don't pay for movers. I know a lot of guys that work for pizza and beer."

"Just so you know, us guys stop doing that around forty. So, take advantage of them while you can."

That must mean he's older than forty. I had him pegged for late thirties. So, we have at least a ten-year age gap. Good to know. Things never work out with men close to my age, so we'll see how this goes. She smiled at Quincy. "Oh, I will."

"I have no doubt." The corner of Quincy's mouth twitched, and he gave a slight shake of his head.

Sorcha suppressed a laugh. She loved noticing his every reaction to her remarks; they made her feel witty and seen.

They reached the door to The Coastal Drip and Quincy opened it, waiting for her to enter.

Sorcha was glad the place was mostly empty. Maybe they could sit and chat for a while. She didn't want the time with Quincy to end. The condo would feel extra lonesome after he left tonight.

She walked to the counter, said hello to the young barista, and ordered a medium iced maple pecan coffee.

Quincy ordered an espresso. Not the plain drip Sorcha was expecting. She smiled, surprised.

"Do you want to sit?" she asked, glancing around the cozy space. There were a handful of tables and several benches along the walls that could be pushed aside when the place hosted open-mic nights.

Quincy's blue eyes held hers. "I'd prefer to sit on the beach."

"That'd be nice, too."

After receiving their beverages and walking back towards the beach, Sorcha asked Quincy about his favorite childhood memory.

"Easy. Camping with my grandfather. He'd take me to the Catskills. It was amazing to get out of the city and breathe fresh air."

"What city did you grow up in?"

"Edison, New Jersey."

"Did your parents ever go with you?"

"No. My dad wasn't around much, and my mom didn't care to go. She couldn't understand the joy of sleeping in a bag on the ground. She preferred her mattress. Comforts of home."

"I can relate to that. I've never been camping."

They'd paused at the crosswalk, waiting for a slow-moving Cadillac to progress through the intersection. The man driving it sat closer to the steering wheel than to his seat back. His hands were high on the wheel, at eleven and one. Maybe this was why Quincy didn't like to drive his motorcycle at night.

"That doesn't surprise me," he said.

She bumped her shoulder against his arm. "Hey now." She tried to interpret that comment. Did he think she was too girly? Pushing her thoughts aside, she continued. "Tell me more about camping. Why did you enjoy it so much?"

"It was quiet, and I felt safe." Quincy took a sip of his coffee before continuing. "Which differed from my home life. My grandpa would make the best bonfires. After the holidays, he'd scrounge around for all the old Christmas lights he could find so he could bring them to throw on the fire when we camped. They'd add pretty colors to the fire. It was fun to watch."

"Not environmentally sound."

"We didn't know that back then. Now they have some chemical packs that do the same thing. I wonder if they're environmentally safe. Anyway, we'd have the best fires and cook hot dogs. Make peasmores."

"Pea what?"

"Pea-smores. S'mores, but with peanut butter and chocolate cups rather than chocolate bars. They are the best. Although making them with Kit Kat bars is pretty good, too."

"That's sacrilege." She stomped her foot. "S'mores are chocolate and marshmallows."

"No, not necessarily. There's no s'more law."

"Hmm, maybe there should be." She puffed out her chest. "I think I'll run for office."

"Ha!" He shook his head. "I don't know who'd vote for you."

"Hey. I have friends and I can influence others."

"I'm sure that's true."

They'd reached Quincy's bike next to the Mockingbird building. "Hold up," he said.

Quincy paused and kicked at his boot. It came off with a little whoosh. Sorcha set her coffee cup on the curb and pulled off her tennis shoes. They placed their shoes and socks on the ground next to the bike and walked onto the sand.

Sorcha looked around for any residents she might recognize. She knew from experience that there wouldn't be many people out after dark, but she usually saw someone she recognized when she went for an evening stroll.

No one tonight.

As they walked towards the surf, Quincy asked about the highs and lows of teaching, and Sorcha shared several highlight stories from this year like the class play she'd directed, and how little Ethan had stolen the show when he belted out an unscripted song in the middle of it. She also shared her heartbreak when one of her favorite students was pulled out of class to be homeschooled.

As she shared these stories, she felt nostalgic, thinking about how her classroom days might be behind her, if she could find a new job before the new school year.

Quincy was a good listener. He asked appropriate questions and didn't talk over her, genuinely listening rather than just waiting for his turn to talk.

For a moment, she considered telling him about her recently discovered inheritance. But she didn't, because she'd start missing her mom, and it would be too easy to get emotional on the beach, in the moonlight, thinking about her mom.

When they returned to the Mockingbird, Sorcha asked Quincy if he wanted to come in for a nightcap, but he declined.

"I make a mean margarita," she said.

"Maybe next time. I don't drink and climb on the bike."

"Wise."

"I like to think I've learned something from my wild youth."

"Well..." She wanted to kiss him, but this was not a date. "Thank you again for the ride. I can mark that off my bucket list."

He raised an eyebrow. "You have a bucket list?"

She laughed. "Don't all thirty-year-olds?"

"No clue. I'd love to hear what else is on it."

"Darn. If only I'd written it down." She pouted at Quincy, and he smiled. "I know a motorcycle ride was on it, though."

"One down. I'm sure I'll see you around?"

"You work tomorrow night?"

"I do."

"I'll see you tomorrow night."

He said good night and climbed on his bike. Sorcha felt another rush of adrenaline as he started the engine.

Back in the condo, she quickly changed into her pajamas and grabbed a small pad of plain paper and some colored pencils she'd found in the game closet. She poured a glass of wine and proceeded to the balcony to sketch the night sky.

Her body thrummed with energy from her evening with Quincy, and she needed to keep her mind and hands busy until she was tired enough for bed.

Tonight, she didn't feel so alone. Looking at the stars and the night sky, she imagined Quincy looking up when he got home. She wondered if his view was like this one. He'd said he couldn't see the Gulf from his house, but he could walk to the beach.

Knowing that they might be looking up at the stars at the same time pushed away the lonely feelings she'd had since coming to Seaside Bay.

Chapter 6

Quincy unlocked the front door to his small one-bedroom rental. It was rundown but held its own charm. Rundown meant reasonable rent, which made it extra charming in Quincy's eyes. He could manage his expenses by working only four or five nights a week.

Though he hadn't gone to college, he figured there was nothing stopping him from learning on his own. He enjoyed reading about world history, economics, science, and mechanics. He'd missed out on the deep discourse that college would have given him, but at least if these subjects came up at the bar, he'd be able to converse without sounding like an uneducated hack.

He'd finally signed up for his first class at the local junior college class this spring. He'd managed to get through the Introduction to Accounting course with a B minus. He'd take it.

Sorcha had mentioned that she was ready for a career change, and while he'd said nothing to her, he was, too.

Twenty-some years of odd jobs, bartending, clerking, hauling, or driving was enough. Normally, he couldn't stomach the idea of working eight hours a day in an office surrounded by two-faced schmucks, but his body was feeling the effects of his middle years, and a desk job was looking more appealing.

Benefits and a retirement plan didn't sound too bad, either. Since he'd soon be taking care of a child, those considerations took on new importance.

Strolling into the bathroom, he stripped and turned on the shower. A quick wash cooled him off and removed the road grime and odor from his body.

Dressed in a clean T-shirt and shorts, he grabbed a glass of water from the sink and headed towards the porch.

This house wasn't much to look at, with its peeling paint and one boarded-up window the landlord swore he'd replace next week. Quincy had been here almost two years, and it remained boarded, so he'd given up expecting it to be fixed.

Even with its problems, Quincy loved the porch with two rocking chairs and a small table. He often sat out there at night and listened to the birds and other wildlife settling in for the evening.

He currently fed a stray dog and two feral cats. He knew he shouldn't, but he couldn't stand seeing the skinny things slinking around cautiously.

"No creature will starve to death on my watch," he muttered to himself as he sat down. The cats were warming up to him so he hoped they might come up tonight and let him pet them.

Rocking gently, Quincy looked to the sky, searching for stars and constellations. Seaside Bay was small enough that there wasn't a lot of light pollution. His house sat half a mile from the main drag, but since trees and shrubs buffered it on all sides, it felt more remote than it actually was. The house sat on half an acre of land, with only a small portion cleared on all sides.

Quincy appreciated the privacy, but wished he had a view of the Gulf from the front porch. There was a small path through the trees and shrubs, and the beach lay only a short distance away. He might startle a few lizards and other reptiles on the way, but he could get there from here.

Noticing the cloud cover, he leaned back and closed his eyes. In his mind, he revisited the evening with Sorcha.

He'd almost backed out of the not-a-date date. It wasn't a good idea. His track record with women was abysmal. And he'd made a deal with himself not to hook up with the pretty ladies that flitted in and out of town on vacations, working on their tans and their wild stories.

But Sorcha had worn him down. She was persistent; he gave her that. And when she finally came up with "let's just hang out as friends, not a date," he'd agreed.

There were so many reasons to say no.

She was too young for him.

She lived four or five states away, depending on the route—he'd checked.

She was too pretty. Too mouthy. Too perfect.

He sighed.

She was perfect.

He wasn't.

She would expect him to say the right thing, buy the right thing, do the right thing. And he wasn't that guy. Sorcha probably daydreamed about a proposal on the beach, with the guy in a light gray suit, and a five-carat ring. She likely fantasized about a Fiji vacation with yacht tours and Michelin-star dining experiences. She would want them to attend galas and functions, and he'd have to buy a tux. He was not a tux-wearing man. They were from two different worlds. Worlds that imploded when they met like a black star swallowing galaxies, not worlds that ignited and made things better.

Besides all of that, he'd just discovered that he had a kid, apparently. This was not the time to get involved with anyone.

"Blast it all," he muttered. He leaned forward and noticed one of the orange cats staring at him from the corner of the porch. "Hey, Gar," he said, noticing its permanently bent ear. The other orange tabby, with two normal ears, he called Field. He thought they might be brothers. They were the same size and had similar markings. The ears were the only way he could tell them apart.

Gar cautiously sidled towards him. Moving slowly, Quincy leaned forward and let his hand dangle so the cat could sniff him. Once he did, he tilted his head towards Quincy's hand. Quincy stroked his fur lightly, not wanting to scare the creature away.

"Finally," he whispered. "Where's your bro, Gar?"

The cat didn't answer but didn't run away, either. Good sign.

"Do you have trouble figuring out the ladies, too? I got girl trouble. Wish you could offer some advice."

The cat turned and arched his back.

"Are you telling me to stay away? You might be onto something."

Gar rushed towards the edge of the porch and jumped off, turning to meow at Quincy after he leapt.

"Forgot to feed 'em," Quincy muttered, standing.

Inside, he scooped dry cat food into a couple of bowls and dry dog food into another. He cracked a couple of eggs and poured them over the dog food. That skinny mutt needed some extra, high-quality protein.

Outside, he called for all three animals. "Gar! Field! Max! Dinner!" He wasn't sure if they were understanding their names yet, but they usually came when he called. He put the bowls on the ground and grabbed the hose to fill the water dishes.

His stray-animal-feeding chores done, he sat on the concrete step and waited.

Just two minutes passed before the cats rounded the corner and streaked to their dishes. He had to wait a few more minutes for the scrawny dog, but when it appeared, Quincy smiled.

"Hey, handsome Max. Good to see you again."

The dog appeared to be part lab and part dachshund with its short legs and long hair. He eyed Quincy as he sidled towards his dish. For the next minute, the dog scarfed down the food.

"Slow down, pup. No one's going to take your food on my watch."

The dog licked his snout, staring at Quincy. But he sat, which gave Quincy a little hope.

"Hey, pup. Good boy. I'm not going to move. I'll sit here and talk quietly. I know you'll tolerate that. Hmm, what to talk about? Well, I took a young woman for a ride tonight. That's not code for anything. Took her for a ride on the motorcycle. She said it was her first time, if you can believe it."

The dog tilted his head from side to side, eyes glued to Quincy.

"It's true. She's something else. So far out of my league. I don't know why she acts interested in me. She's beautiful and smart. Educated. She must have all kinds of guys sniffing around her. I know there aren't many single men under sixty in this little town, but there are some."

Quincy noticed the cats had finished eating and had moved under a large shrub near the rusted storage shed.

Eying the shed, he thought about Eva Lyn. There were several dangers in this yard that hadn't bothered him until now. Rusted metal, overgrown shrubs, stray animals. His eyes darted back to the stray dog. Would it attack a child? Quincy wouldn't give it a chance. No way would she be out here and not within arm's reach.

He added 'safe play area' to the list of considerations for his next rental.

Moving away meant he wouldn't see Sorcha again. *That's for the best.*

She made him want things a guy like him shouldn't want.

Chapter 7

Waiting for Linda to answer the phone, Sorcha pulled a bottle of iced tea from the fridge. She needed a little caffeine to get her day started. She wanted to bake chocolate chip cookies for Quincy before the day got too hot.

Linda answered on the fourth ring. "Sorry, I was on the phone with my mother. She's up in arms because there's not enough stuff on my registry, as she puts it."

"Tsk, tsk, Linda Lu. whatever will you do?"

Linda laughed. "End up with kitchen gadgets I don't need and won't use. How are things going in the Sunshine State?"

"It's getting interesting."

She thought about her evening with Quincy. She could not wait to tell her friend about it. Linda would help her sort out her feelings.

"Yeah? Tell me more."

"Spent some time with the handsome Quincy last night."

"I thought you did that on the regular. Sitting on a barstool, I mean."

"No, I saw him outside of Crabbie's. I talked him into taking me on a motorcycle ride."

"Is that the only ride he took you on?"

"Yes, of course. Though I wouldn't mind more. He's hesitant. He said he would not go on a 'date' with me but will hang out as friends."

"And you agreed? That's not like you."

Sorcha held the phone against her shoulder while she pulled two cookie sheets out of the cabinet. "I know. A first for everything."

"Did you have fun?"

"It was nice. Little ride. Little walk. Some coffee and a friendly chat."

"Great. Think there will be more?"

"I don't know. He's working tonight, and I told him I'd stop in. I promised to bake cookies and take them to him. That was the deal for taking me on the ride. But I wish I knew a way to keep things going. Maybe have a proper date."

"If that's what you want." Linda sounded doubtful.

"It is! I just don't know how to make it happen." She reached for a mixing bowl.

"What if you flirt with other men in the bar? You know. Make him jealous. I've seen you use that ploy to your advantage before."

"Yes." Sorcha nodded, though Linda couldn't see her. "But I don't want to tick Quincy off. He's not the kind that will tolerate foolish games."

"Well, just keep being yourself, Sor'. He'd be a fool not to fall for you. You're the best!"

Sorcha smiled. "Thanks, friend. I needed that."

"It's true. And I know you love a challenge in relationships. It seems like Quincy is the ultimate challenge."

"He may be. I do like a challenge."

"Well, challenge away. What else is happening besides Quincy? Come to any career decisions?"

"No. I've got a nice tan, though."

"I expected no less."

"I will become a bronzed goddess after spending another week down here."

"You're always a goddess."

Sorcha laughed. "Hopefully, my tan won't fade before your wedding."

"You'll only be home for two weeks before the wedding. You'll be fine."

"If you say so," Sorcha replied. She grabbed an apple out of the refrigerator. "Hey, is it too late to add a plus-one to the wedding?"

"Quincy?"

"I thought I would ask him, but if it's too late, I understand."

"It's a casual wedding on a public beach. It will be fine. Do you think he'll come?"

Sorcha rinsed the apple under the sink and shook it off. "I'm not sure. Might need to be more convincing."

"If you dig it, do it. Well, I should get going. Only four weeks to go, and I have a lot of loose ends to tie up. What are your plans for the day?"

"I'm meeting my new friends, Rosalie and Winnie, at the pool for some fun in the sun."

"Rosie and Winnie?"

"Rosalie, hun." Sorcha mimicked the name Rosalie called her. "Rosalie lives in the building. Winnie is visiting. They are both eighty-two years old. They've been friends for seventy years. Can you believe it? They're a riot. I met them at Crabbie's the other night."

"Wow. Seventy years, that's amazing."

"They're fantastic. They've seen it all, done it all, got all the T-shirts. I think they're my fairy godmothers. I met them the night I talked Quincy into seeing me outside the bar. They might have instigated the whole thing."

Linda laughed. "Oh, my. I hope I get to meet them when I come."

"I told them about your wedding. They may think they have an invitation."

"Hey, now. A plus-one is fine, but you can't invite the entire town!"

"Hmm. Just the building?"

"I've got to go. Try not to invite the entire building."

Sorcha had no intention of inviting the entire building, but Quincy was definitely on the list.

Quincy waited for his mom to answer her phone. The ringing made him want to knock his head against the wall.

He wasn't used to calling his family for help, but he needed someone now.

Eva Lyn would arrive in less than a week, and he couldn't take care of a child on his own.

He'd already called his sister Lainey. She was shocked but delighted to hear that she had a niece. She sympathized with Quincy's situation, but she couldn't take the time to visit. Her kids, Zach and Mattie, were athletes with multiple games, tournaments and other kid activities—Quincy tuned her out after ten minutes of describing Zach's traveling-baseball schedule—and there was no way she could help. She'd be available via phone to answer questions, but that was all the help she could give.

His mother answered on the third ring. "Quincy? What's wrong?"

He rolled his eyes. He should call more often. "Hey, Ma. Nothing's wrong." Everything was wrong. "Don't worry."

"Whew. You scared me. What's up?"

He heard the clinking of dishes and pictured her at the sink, washing dishes. He glanced at the clock; it was one. Lunch dishes. She worked the second shift at a medical device manufacturing plant and would prepare to leave soon. He couldn't remember what they made now; the assembly line changed every few months.

"I know you don't have a lot of time, but I have some big news to share."

"News? Are you moving back?"

The excitement in her voice gave him pause. He knew she hated the fact that both her kids lived so far away. "No, Mom. I won't move back. You know that."

He'd told her a dozen times that once he left, he wouldn't return. There were too many painful memories.

She sighed. "Yeah, yeah. Why'd ya call?"

"I recently found out that..." He took a deep breath.

"You've got the cancer." Her pronunciation of cancer didn't include an "r" sound, it ended in an "a".

"No! I'm not sick." He'd just blurt it out. "I have a kid."

"You're having a baby? With who?"

"Not having. Have. The baby is almost eighteen months old. I haven't met her yet."

"Her? A little girl? Who? How? Where?"

He chuckled. So many questions. "The mother was a woman I dated in Myrtle Beach."

"Was?"

"She died. Overdose."

"Died? Is the baby addicted?"

He had no idea. Would an addicted baby have issues a year and a half later? He hadn't thought to ask Ms. Myer about that. "I don't think so." He comforted himself by assuming the social worker would have brought that up.

"Gracious! Well, what do you know?"

He heard her light a cigarette and take a deep inhale.

"My name is on the birth certificate, so the social worker assumes it's mine. I can have a paternity test. But..." He paused. "The baby's name is Eva Lyn. I know that doesn't prove anything, but Leeza, the baby's mother, knew what Grandma meant to me. I guess she named the baby after her."

"Oh. Well. Do you have a picture?"

He hadn't thought of asking for one. "No. Not yet. She'll be here next Thursday. I'll take one and send it to you right away."

"Another grandbaby. Can't wait to tell the girls at work. Just wish I could meet her."

This could be the door. "Well, that's why I called. What's your vacation schedule look like? I'd pay for your flight down here. I could really use some help. Already asked Lainey, and she can't make it."

"Oh, Quincy. I don't know. I'm so close to retirement. If I take any days off, it just postpones my retirement date. Right now, I'm scheduled to retire on October first. I just want to be done. This job is breaking my body down. I have to take three Aleve before I even walk through the door at work. Standing, moving my hands constantly. I want to be retired."

"Hey, I get it. Don't worry about it. I'll figure something out." I *always do*.

"Yes, you will. Oh, I wanted to tell you, I heard that Blaze Parsen died. In prison, of course. Not sure of the details but wanted to pass that along."

"All right."

Blaze Parsen, the man who'd shot and killed his old man on the sidewalk outside of their house. Blaze had called Pete out to talk, but hadn't given him a chance to speak.

Quincy had run out of the house at the sound of the gunshot. Blaze hadn't missed. His steady hand had sent the bullet through Pete's heart.

"At least our taxes are no longer supporting him," Janice said.

"There's that." Quincy ran his hand over his beard. "Gonna let you go. I've got to find some help."

"OK. Send me that picture as soon as you can."

He hung up and looked at the notebook on the table. He'd made a list to organize his thoughts: call his sister; call his mom; find a sitter. He shook his head.

A burning sensation pulsed through his gut. It'd been months since he'd thought about Blaze. Or his dad. He stood and poured himself a glass of milk.

Glancing out the kitchen window, he allowed the memories to come. He'd learned that it was better to look at those memories, face them, and take the heartache that they brought. Far better than avoiding them. When he did that, he usually woke in a pool of sweat, unable to remember the nightmares.

Once he felt the tightness in his chest loosen, he spent thirty minutes searching on his phone for babysitters in the surrounding area. He even broke down and joined Facebook because he'd heard that it was a good place to ask locals for recommendations.

The problem with moving frequently and not wanting to make real friends was that he didn't have a community of support. The closest thing he had was his team of coworkers at Crabbie's. Jasmyn didn't have kids, and Lloyd, the barback, probably had a dozen, but didn't claim any of them. Quincy didn't know Tania well, but he knew she had a kid, so he hoped she'd be able to answer some questions. The only downside was that he'd have to admit that he had a kid and hadn't been told about it until now. How's that for Father of the Year? What kind of guy are you when the baby's mother doesn't even attempt to tell you about your child?

Leeza had not been stable. She'd preferred drugs over anything else, but he'd been blind to her addiction at first. She'd been charming and funny, and she'd made him feel valued by always complimenting him and thanking him for the littlest things.

After his failed marriage, her encouragement had been a boost to his shattered ego. Shaking his head, he told himself he needed to stop thinking about Leeza and start thinking about the toddler who would come to him in a few days. He needed a plan, and it wouldn't happen while he was thinking about the past. He needed to concentrate on the here and now. On Eva Lyn. If he was lucky, he might get to think about the future.

Chapter 8

Sorcha strolled into the bar, excited to see Quincy, hoping the short time together the night before had softened him towards her.

She wasn't sure why she was so fascinated by him. He was completely unlike any other guy she'd dated. She usually went for the boy-next-door, frat-guy types. But that hadn't worked out so well, so why not try something new? Something tall, dark, and dangerous.

All right, not dangerous, but dangerous-looking. She knew he was a softy underneath the tattoos, sour looks, and gruff voice. There was a heart of gold under that tight black T-shirt, and she was here to mine for it. First, she'd mine a glass of chardonnay. Liquid gold.

Quincy was standing behind the bar, wiping the counter with a white rag in a slow, languid motion, talking to a customer who wore an offensive ball-cap that Sorcha ignored. Quincy glanced over his shoulder at her and slid his eyes to the far end of the bar, suggesting she sit away from the man he was talking to.

She proceeded to the spot Quincy indicated, placed the container of cookies on the bar, and slid onto a stool, pulling her shorts down so her legs wouldn't stick to the seat. Wrapping the thin shoulder strap of her cross-body bag around the purse and setting it on the bar, she pulled her cell phone out of her pocket and placed it in front of her. She was determined to get a picture of Quincy tonight, unsure if he would be a willing participant, so she wanted the phone close to snap a picture when she got the chance.

Finally, Quincy walked towards her. His lips hitched in a half-smile, which would intimidate most women, but not Sorcha. She was here to conquer and control, or at least kiss.

"You again?" he asked, sliding over a Crabbie's drink coaster.

"Yes. Aren't you lucky? Look, I brought your cookies."

"Lucky? We'll see." He picked up the container, peeled up a corner of the lid, taking a sniff. "Smells great. Thank you. What're you having?"

"A chardonnay, please."

"Can I share the cookies?" When she nodded, he pulled the lid off and set the container on the bar. She watched as he proceeded to the cooler, grabbed the bottle, and poured her a glass, his muscular arms straining the limits of his shirt sleeves.

Placing the glass down, he crossed his arms and leaned against the far side of the bar. Luckily, there were few patrons in the bar, and the volume of the music wasn't so high that they had to shout at each other.

"So," he started, "how was your day lying in the sun, eating chips?"

"I didn't get to lay in the sun all day, since I promised to make someone cookies." She smiled at Quincy.

"I appreciate your sacrifice."

She tilted her head in acknowledgment. "I think this will be my first and only solo vacation. Gawh!" She threw her hands in the air. "It's so boring. I didn't bring supplies to work on my side hustle. I was trying to do the full vacation experience. Alone."

"Bookmark the side-hustle comment. We'll come back to that. But I thought you were trying to sort out your future. Make any progress there?"

"No. A short list of ideas, but no solid plans. It's gettin' ridiculous. I should just accept that I will be a teacher for the rest of my life."

"I thought you liked teaching."

"I like it, yes, a lot. But I'm ready for a new challenge."

"Well, I can't help you out very much on the career advice. I haven't mastered that area myself."

"I bet you have a long list of different occupations on your resumé." She took a drink of the wine, the cool liquid sliding languidly down her throat.

"What's a resumé again?"

"Ha. Do you need help to put one together? I actually do pretty good with those. I'm a natural bologna maker."

"No. I'm pretty good with the BS myself," he said. "Normally, I just apply for jobs, fill out applications. They don't ask for a resumé."

"Is bartending your favorite job?" She appreciated he had time to talk to her, but she'd hoped they could talk about something other than work.

"It's all right. Get to meet some interesting...people." He widened his eyes as he leaned towards her. "Hours are rough, though. Tips are unreliable. But I'm not complaining."

"Do you want to do something else?" Sorcha knew he was a drifter who moved a lot.

"I do. Not sure what, though. Or where."

He glanced away, and Sorcha wondered where his mind had drifted. The troubled look knitting his eyebrows bothered her. To change the mood, she asked, "Have you considered stripping? I hear they make great tips." She held her hands out wide, like she was measuring something.

"Not even in my younger years would I do that. Now, no one wants to see a forty-year-old strip."

Ah ha! He was vague about his age the other day. "So, you're forty? Good to know."

"Forty-three. I rounded."

She would have told her students to round forty-three up to forty-five, but she would not mention that to Quincy. She looked down at her glass, placing the fingertips of both hands on the base, and scooting it back and forth. At least she'd had time to paint her nails today. The bubblegum pink color matched her large, dangling earrings perfectly. "OK, no stripping. Got it. Construction?"

"Done it. Don't care to do it again."

"Sales? Cars? Motorcycles? Real estate?"

"You have to deal with people."

"You deal with people here."

"Yes, but I'm giving them what they want. Not trying to up-sell them. No quotas to meet here."

She nodded. "That's legit. Truck driver?"

"Can't stand driving for hours on end. Unless it's on my bike."

"Noted. You've got me stumped, Q. Usually I'm pretty good at brainstorming and problem solving."

"Bet you're good at a lot of things."

He gave her a look that might pass as suggestive, but Sorcha wouldn't assume. Plus, she would not make things easy for Quincy. If he was interested, he would need to do a little wooing.

"Maybe so."

Another man slid onto a stool further down the bar and Quincy walked over to fill his order. After bringing the man his bottle and some quick chitchat, Quincy was back in front of Sorcha.

"What about your career options? What are you thinking?" he asked.

"I don't know. I've done several side hustles over the years, but nothing I can turn into a full-time gig."

"Yeah? Like what?"

"I've made jewelry. T-shirts, sweatshirts. Book sleeves. Um, what else? Oh yeah, I crocheted blankets, but they were pricey to ship."

"Did not have you pegged for an arts and crafts girlie."

"I love art." She thought about her mom and their trips to the Art Institute in Chicago when she was a kid. They would take the train to the city, have lunch, browse the museum and shop in the gift shop. She cherished every moment of those trips.

"Yeah?"

"Yeah. But it's hard to translate that love into a career. I would need an advanced degree to teach art history or to become a curator in a museum or to run an art gallery. Besides, I just paid off my college student loans. I'm not looking to get into that mess again."

Quincy nodded. "Understood."

"I think doing something you love, like art, as your full-time job can kill the love for it in the long run," she continued, "so I'll keep to my love of art as a hobby and interest instead of making a career out of it."

"That's logical."

She sighed. "So, as you can see, one week of my vacation is over, and I still haven't figured out what's next. The only good news is, I have a job that I can go back to in August if nothing comes up. But I really want something to come up."

Quincy chuckled. "I can tell."

A group of several couples entered the bar and began pulling a few high-top tables together. Sorcha watched the dynamics and smiled to see one man standing at the far end of the tables shouting directions to the others to get the tables just right. Bossy.

She glanced at Quincy and rolled her eyes.

"I'd better get over there and take their orders. It's going to get busy in here."

He left, and Sorcha thought about their discussion. They were both at a crossroads in life, looking for something new. Too bad he said he wasn't interested in dating. She had another week remaining in Florida and she was hoping for some fun. A distraction. Quincy might be both.

Rosalie and Winnie came in and sat down next to Sorcha. Quincy was glad Sorcha would have company if he got busy.

Being Friday night, it was likely to get busy. Even though this was a heavy retirement area, many of the retirees had kids and grandkids and great-grandkids who liked to visit and take advantage of the beautiful beaches.

Rosalie and Winnie ordered their drinks and began telling Sorcha about their shopping escapades.

He served their drinks, and other patrons began filing in. It was after dinner; time for things to pick up.

He'd been serving drinks steadily and noticed the dance floor filling up. There was a Jimmy Buffett tune playing. He smiled when he noticed Sorcha and her companions make their way through the crowd. Sorcha grasped the hands of both women, leading the way. Shuffling to the center of the floor, Sorcha began laughing at something Winnie had said. Her head tilted to the side, causing her straight blond hair to brush across her smooth shoulder. He wanted to look away, but she was captivating. A drunk kid, young enough that Quincy had carded him, came up, demanding another beer. Quincy wanted to cut him off, but that would take too much energy. He'd already asked and knew the people with this kid were monitoring him. He'd be alright.

When his eyes swung back to the dance floor, he quickly found Sorcha holding court. Her hands in the air, her hips swaying back and forth.

She looked his way and smiled. He nodded, looking away. She wasn't hiding her intentions. He'd seen a hundred women like Sorcha. On vacation, find the bartender attractive, try to seduce him so she could take a fun memory home with her.

He wasn't having it.

It had been different in his twenties. He'd thought nothing of leaving the bar with a different woman most nights, but after his failed marriage to Suze and other failed relationships, he'd decided his ability to choose the right woman was broken. And that wasn't the only thing broken about him.

He was just broken. Didn't deserve love and happiness. Wouldn't know what to do with it if it hit him in the face. It was better to ride solo. No hassles. No regrets. No complications. His daughter would be here in a few days, and that was the only complication he could handle.

What in the world was he going to do? He'd asked his coworkers to cover his shifts for a week after Eva Lyn arrived, but that was the best he could do. He'd need a babysitter after that.

Too bad Seaside Bay was a small retirement community. There were no daycare centers in town; the nearest was twenty minutes away. It might do in a pinch, but he had decided that having a sitter come to his house was better, especially until Eva Lyn settled in. Her world had already turned upside down. He didn't want to put her in a daycare with a dozen other kids and tired caregivers.

He grabbed a beer for a man at the bar and tossed down coasters for a young couple who'd pulled up seats and were actually looking at the drink specials card, saying they would need a minute or two to make a choice. Glancing towards the dance floor, he noticed that Sorcha was dancing with a friend of the drunk kid.

Fine. It'd give Quincy time to wash the dishes. As he filled the sink with hot, soapy water, he thought about baby bottles. Would the social worker bring any with her? Would she bring clothes and other supplies? Maybe he could get his sister up here for a day to help him shop for baby things. No, she'd said she would be in Tennessee this weekend for a baseball tournament. He shook his head as he washed glasses with vigor. How was he going to shop with a kid? Even more concerning was his motorcycle!

He couldn't attach a baby seat to his bike. He was going to need to get a car before she arrived. Thankfully, he had money saved. He hoped he could find a quality used car for a few thousand dollars. Ha. Not likely.

He asked the new couple for their order and made their drinks.

How am I going to get to a car dealership? Tampa's too far for a rideshare.

Sorcha deposited her boy toy back at his table and approached the bar, laughing with Winnie and Rosalie. They sat down and Sorcha lifted her hair off the back of her neck and fanned herself. "Whoa, I'm hot."

Was he supposed to agree with her? "You ladies need another drink?" he asked.

"Just water for me," Sorcha said. Winnie and Rosalie still had their beverages and said no to refills.

Quincy paused the mojito he was working on and poured a glass of ice water for Sorcha.

"Thank you!" she exclaimed.

He grunted.

"I think I have a new dance buddy." She took a long sip from the water. "He is kind of hot, don't you think?"

"He looks like a piece of..."

"Quincy!" Rosalie said. Sorcha raised an eyebrow.

"Work." He grounded out between clenched teeth.

Sorcha shook her head. "He was funny and sweet. And—"

"Not listening."

Quincy finished the mixed drinks and placed them in front of the couple on the opposite side of the bar. He wanted to engage them in some witty conversation and ignore Sorcha, but they started making out and he turned away in disgust.

He checked in with all the customers sitting at the bar, but no one needed anything. He picked up empty bottles and glasses.

Seeing nothing else to do, he went back to the sink to finish washing. Unfortunately, the sink was right across from Sorcha and the silver-haired ladies. It was almost like she'd planned to be in his eyesight as much as possible. He thought about his predicament. He needed a car, which would require getting both his bike and a car back from Tampa, assuming he could find something passable during the first outing. Looking at Sorcha, who was typing on her phone, an idea formed. She'd been on his bike once. She wasn't too squirmy. If she went with him to look for a car, she could drive the car back, following him on his bike. She was on vacation and kept complaining that she was bored. She might go for it. If he asked for her help, he'd have to tell her why he needed a car. Was that such a bad thing? Once she knew he had a kid, her interest in him would speed away faster than a souped-up bike on the Bonneville Salt Flats in Utah.

She put her phone down, asked for another glass of wine, and offered to buy a round for Rose and Winnie. They took her up on her offer. He quickly made their drinks. Here was his chance.

"Hey, do you have plans for tomorrow afternoon?"

"Besides working on my tan? No. Why?"

"I could use a little help. I need to go car shopping. If I'm lucky enough to find one, I won't be able to get both it and my bike back at the same time. Would you mind taking a ride with me? And if I find a car, would you drive it back home?"

"Really?" She raised an eyebrow like she was appraising him. "Where are you going to get a car? Did you find one online?"

"No, but the place where I get my bike serviced has a used car lot, and I trust the guys that run the place. I think I can find something there."

"Why do you need a car? I thought you liked your bike."

"I love it. But I need a car."

"Why?" she persisted.

He glanced around the bar. Rosalie and Winnie were deep in conversation. He'd probably be interrupted five times before he could finish the story, and he didn't want to spill his private business with a crowd around.

"I'll tell you tomorrow."

She made a quick humming sound in her throat. "All right, Mr. Q. I'll help you out, but I want something in return."

"What?"

"Another non-date date. Some time to hang out together outside of this place."

"We'll hang out tomorrow, shopping for a car."

"No. Other than that."

Once she knew why he needed to buy a car, she'd spin off like a loose wheel. "Fine. If you still want that after tomorrow, we'll figure something out."

She beamed at him. Her smile warmed him in places it shouldn't. She was so far out of his league. He needed to shut down the feelings she stirred up. He didn't have a chance with her long-term, and he couldn't start anything short-term. As of Thursday, he'd be a full-time single dad. Not the kind of guy a lady like Sorcha would be interested in.

Sorcha leaned forward. "So, what time will you pick me up?"

"One."

"Okay. Sounds great. I'll be ready to go for a ride."

Did she always speak in double entendres or was that his imagination? He turned away to make the rounds again. He imagined the look of horror on her face when he told her about the baby girl. She'd be mortified and disgusted and would probably book a flight home even earlier than planned.

That was fine. He wouldn't even have time to pursue her once the kid arrived. His hands would be full. He prayed he could make some progress on a sitter by this weekend.

His footsteps faltered, and he turned slowly, looking back at Sorcha. She was a teacher. Younger kids. Not babies, but she was a woman. Didn't baby care come naturally to them? Maybe he could convince her to babysit while she was here. Probably just more wishful thinking, but he'd have to take a chance. He was desperate.

Chapter 9

Sorcha climbed onto the motorcycle behind Quincy, less nervous this time, since she knew what to expect. At least regarding the trip to Tampa. Why Quincy needed a car suddenly was still unclear. The ride wasn't conducive to talking, so she had to wait to ask.

During the ride, she hung on tight, wrapping her arms around him, squeezing her body against his, and watching for glimpses of the Gulf. When they reached the used car lot, her body vibrated as she climbed off the motorcycle. She pulled the helmet off and handed it to Quincy, who set it on the seat as he asked if she enjoyed the ride.

"It's a lot of fun," she said as she finger-combed her hair. She could feel a few knots towards the ends.

"Good." He started looking around the lot. "Hope I can find something reliable and inexpensive."

Here was her opening. "So, why are you buying a car? I thought you were happy with the bike."

"I love my bike. I won't get rid of it, but I need a car."

"Need?"

Quincy stopped walking and turned towards her. His eyes dropped from hers quickly, and he looked at the ground, kicking a small rock aside.

"I can't put a baby seat on the back of the bike," he said, raising his eyes to hers.

Sorcha laughed. "Of course not. That's ridiculous. Wait, a baby seat. Why would you need that? Are you babysitting as a side gig?" The idea was ridiculous, but she had to throw it out there.

"No. Being a dad is about to become my full-time gig."

"Full-time dad?" Did she hear him right? "I didn't think you had a girlfriend..."

"I don't."

Bells seemed to clang in her ears. This was the most shocking thing he could have said to her. She shook her head to focus on Quincy's face. The lines across his brow looked deeper than they had last night. "But you're having a baby," she prompted.

"I have a baby. An eighteen-month-old."

"Wow." Sorcha felt her eyes widen. "You could have told me that."

"I didn't know until a week ago."

"What? You're not serious. How did you not know? I don't understand."

Quincy sighed. "I've had a little time to adjust to the news. Sorry to spring it on you. I received a call telling me a former girlfriend had my child but never told me about it. Unfortunately, the mother passed away, and Child Protective Services tracked me down. I'm next of kin and they couldn't find anyone else to take her in."

"Her?" Sorcha pictured pink bows and little dresses.

"Yes, her. She's arriving on Thursday, and the first order of business is to get a car. There's other stuff I need to get, and having a car will help me haul it home."

"Wow. Yes, I can see that. It would be comical seeing you go down the road with a giant crib box tied onto your back. Though I bet you would figure out a way to manage it."

Quincy smiled, but it didn't reach his eyes.

"Hey," she asked, "how are you feeling about this? Excited? Shocked? Frightened?"

"All the above. But let's save that conversation for later. Right now, I need to find a car."

Sorcha followed him up and down the aisles until Quincy found a black, four-door Chevy Impala that he liked, with low mileage and a decent price tag. She was shocked to see him offer cash for the car.

After a test drive and completed paperwork, Quincy asked her to follow him back to his place. She was excited that she was going to get to see his home and to find out more about the life-changing event about to take place there.

Quincy kept a close eye on Sorcha behind him, making sure she kept up, and hoping she didn't have any problems with the car. As he pulled in front of his house, she parked behind him. When she got out of the car and handed him the keys, he asked, "How was the drive?"

"Good. No issues." She shrugged. "I think it's a good one. Hope it's reliable for you."

"Thanks." He gestured towards the house. "I'll give you the tour and we can sit on the porch."

The tour was quick; there wasn't a lot to see. But Sorcha was very complimentary about the limited decor and neatness of the place. He grabbed a beer for her and a glass of water for himself. Sorcha walked outside ahead of him and took the chair in the corner. It was far enough over on the east side of the porch that it had a tiny view of the water.

"This is nice," she said, gazing through the trees towards the Gulf.

"It's quiet. That's my favorite part. It was a good find."

"So, you rent."

"I do. Told you, I travel light. Look for furnished places to live. Less of a headache, less responsibility…"

"Fewer mementos."

"That, too."

"So, you're about to be a full-time dad. How's that going to work?"

Quincy shook his head. "Honestly? No idea. I've called my mom and my sister, and neither of them can come to help. So, I need to find a nanny, or at least a solid sitter. I still need to go shopping for baby stuff and don't know what I'm doing."

"I can help with shopping! That's my thing! Born to shop. And..." She paused. "I'm a girl. I love shopping for baby things."

"Have much experience?"

"Some. Baby showers. I'm a frequent guest. I'm at that age..."

He waited to see if she would say more. Did she want to have kids someday? Or was she content going to showers? Regardless, he could use the help.

Watching Sorcha stare off towards the water did something to Quincy. It was easy to imagine her being there for him as he undertook this additional responsibility, but he had no right even to imagine it. She would go home soon, fall in love with the right sort of man who was better for her. Someone who didn't have a kid. Someone who had a proper job. Someone who would help her pick out the perfect house with a white picket fence. Someone who would give her her own child, not someone else's. A girlfriend would host her baby shower, and she'd be loaded with gifts and joy and whatever else happened at those things.

Quincy cleared his throat to pull her out of her reverie. And his. His thoughts weren't doing him any good.

"What are you doing tomorrow?" he asked.

She smiled at him, that partial smile that drove him crazy. "Hmm, I'll have to check my busy, busy calendar. Why do you ask?"

"Want to go shopping?"

"Heck, yeah!"

Chapter 10

Sorcha ran a hand over the soft fleece blanket, smiling at the pink bunnies and purple bows on the cream background. She wanted to toss it in the cart but hesitated. Quincy needed necessities, and the forty-dollar blanket was too extravagant.

She'd spent hours Saturday night processing her shock at Quincy's news. She'd tried to call Linda to talk about it, but Linda was at dinner and couldn't talk. Once the initial shock wore off, Sorcha considered Quincy's situation. He was not one to complain or talk about his feelings, but he wore his apprehension in the lines on his face. It didn't alter her feelings about him. If anything, it made him even more attractive. Yes, he'd had more time to accept the news than Sorcha, but she'd seen him every day this week, and he didn't seem to struggle or be distracted. He'd handled himself like she'd always seen him do. Stoic. Aloof. He'd bought a car, and he was shopping for baby things. He'd manned up and was going to be a dad. Some men didn't have it in themselves to do that. She admired that about him.

She looked at the list in her hand. They'd found a crib, high chair, and a stroller—the highest priority items—and Quincy had left to load those large items into his car before focusing on clothes and accessories. Sorcha was getting a head start, filling the cart with bath items, bottles, diapers, and several toys. She'd told Quincy that she would hit a few thrift stores and secondhand-clothing stores for kids. She knew she'd be able to find good quality outfits for a fraction of retail prices.

"You've made progress," Quincy said, glancing at her cart.

"The list helps. Got everything loaded?"

"Yes. And room for more. The trunk is deeper than it looked."

"Good, because I've found a few things."

"I see. Are we done?"

Quincy looked worn out. Not only was shopping not his thing, he was also spending a lot of money on a child he hadn't even met yet.

Sorcha reached out, placing her hand on his forearm. "I'm afraid not. There are a few more things on the list. But do you want to take a break? Go get a coffee and have a sit?"

"No. Let's get what we still need. We can grab dinner on the way home."

He was determined. Sorcha smiled at him. "Won't take too much more time. We need to get some blankets, crib sheets, and a diaper bag. Then we can call it done."

He pointed to the large package of diapers in the cart. "There's a diaper bag."

She shook her head and laughed. "Those are the diapers. A diaper bag is what you use to carry them around, along with bottles, and clean clothes, and burp rags. And..."

He held his hands up. "I got it. I got it. Yes, we need that. Lead the way."

Quincy made quick decisions, and soon they were on the way to dinner. They stopped at a barbecue restaurant, and after placing their orders, they found a table on the deck overlooking the beach and the Gulf.

"Hey," Quincy said, taking a sip of the beer he'd ordered. "Thank you again for going shopping with me today. I don't know what I would've done without you."

"It was my pleasure. Seriously. I love to shop."

He smiled. "I noticed."

"I'm looking forward to shopping for baby clothes. Thanks for trusting me to do that."

"You'll do a much better job of it than I would." He let out a long sigh and shook his head. "What am I going to do? I'm not prepared for this. I'm going to ruin this kid's life."

The server, a pretty young woman with kind eyes, brought their plates of food, and Sorcha bit her tongue, saving what she wanted to say until the server left.

As soon as the young lady walked away, Sorcha leaned forward and put her hand on Quincy's arm. "Stop that right now. No, you're not. Men become fathers for the first time every day, and they manage just fine. You're going to figure it out. It will be bumpy, but you're going to do great. I know it."

"I wish I had your confidence. It's just that I never pictured myself in this position. Even if I had considered parenthood, which I haven't, I would have had time to adjust. Months, while the mother was pregnant, at least. Now this." He chomped down on a fry. "I'm getting less than two weeks to prepare. Not only do I not know how to take care of a kid, I have a full-time job, with no partner to help. The schedule is going to be a problem. I can't take a kid into the bar while I work."

He took a bite of his brisket sandwich and shook his head.

Sorcha yearned to comfort him. That he was so worried about it meant he'd be fine, but he couldn't see that yet. He needed some experience under his belt, and then he'd be a good father; she was confident of that.

"Lucky for you, I'm here and available."

"What? Are you sure?"

The look of surprise and hope in his eyes tugged at Sorcha's heart. She was already in danger of falling for this man. Knowing that he needed her—that he and his daughter needed her—was too much.

She thought about her upcoming flight home and wondered what it would take to change her ticket. Would Linda's family let her stay even longer in their condo?

Having a little inheritance money waiting for her helped ease the financial guilt.

If Quincy asked, she could reasonably stay the summer and help take care of his daughter.

It might slow down her career decision. How could she job hunt while she was in Florida? Unless she got serious about a remote position.

These thoughts flew through her mind even as she nodded at Quincy. "Of course. You need me, tough guy."

"That I do." He leaned closer and put an arm around her back in a casual side hug. "Thank you."

Sorcha closed her eyes and leaned into him. His arm around her was grounding. She wanted to wrap her arms around him and squeeze him, but refrained.

At home, Quincy felt some of his anxiety ease. He'd been here long enough that this place had become home, his sanctuary.

They unloaded the purchases into the middle of the living room and set about sorting and organizing.

Sorcha insisted on washing the blankets and bedding back at her place, so they put those items in a large shopping bag and placed it by the door.

"The good news is you don't have a lot of clutter; the bad news is you only have one bedroom. Where are you planning to put everything?" Sorcha looked around the sparsely furnished living room, her hands resting on her hips. She wore a pink dress that flattered her curves. The dress had distracted him several times during their shopping trip. When he'd come back into the store and found her snuggling a baby blanket, his mind played tricks on him. He'd felt like they were in an actual relationship for one moment. He shook his head to dislodge that memory. *She's just helping because she pities you. Don't start thinking she actually cares about you.*

"The crib will go in the corner in my bedroom. A changing table next to it. Playpen in here. What else?"

"Are you going to need a dresser for your daughter's clothes?" Sorcha spun towards him. "Wait a minute! I don't even know her name!"

"Right." Quincy ran his hand over his head. "The social worker said her name is Eva Lyn."

"That's pretty."

"And meaningful."

"Oh?"

"It was my grandmother's name. My ex must have remembered it when the baby was born. Maybe she knew it'd be easier for me to feel a connection if the name was meaningful to me."

"Wow. I still can't believe she never reached out to tell you."

"I left no forwarding address, and I blocked her phone number when I left town." He sat on the end of the cracked leather sofa and motioned for her to sit as well. She chose the other end of the sofa. "We didn't date very long. I didn't introduce her to any of my family, never even told her the names of the cities where my mom and sister live, so she would've had to work hard to track them down. They don't even have the same last name as me; they're both married. So, I'm not surprised she never told me."

"And she died?"

"She was a drug user, and I assume that contributed to her death, but I don't know for sure yet. Once I found out about the drugs I was gone."

"Wow. That's scary. Do you know if your daughter has any health issues from that?"

"Don't know." Quincy shook his head. Both his mom and Sorcha had thought of asking that. He hadn't. "I'm hoping the woman will go over that stuff when she brings her. Do you want to be here when she arrives? Maybe you'll think to ask other questions I won't think of."

"Do you really want me here? This is a momentous occasion."

"I know it is, and yes."

"But you don't really know me." She leaned towards him, resting a hand on the cushion between them.

"I need a friend, and you've been a friend to me. You've helped me out of two jams already."

"I don't mind. It's been fun getting to know you, mystery Q."

"Mystery Q?"

"I've called you that for a while. You're brooding and quiet. You're a mystery."

"Well, you're no open book."

"That's because you're quiet and don't ask a lot of questions. I'd be happy to tell you most anything. Though you'll probably find me pretty boring. I'm a schoolteacher who's never been married. Live with my best friend—at least until she gets married and moves in with her new husband. Other than going out to bars and concerts, I like to make things, do crafts, be artistic."

"Here I thought you were a party animal always looking for your next hook-up."

"False. I like to have a good time, but I'm more of a homebody than a party girl. One of these days, some lucky guy is going to fall madly in love with me and sweep me off my feet. We'll marry and have pretty babies. Buy a cute little house and settle down. The American dream."

"That American dream is getting harder to achieve." He thought about his own situation, suddenly discovering he was a dad with a toddler. "But I expected those goals from you. Like I said, you're going to go home, find a guy with a steady job and good health benefits, fall in love, and start having your own babies."

"I don't know why you keep insisting that I must be *home* to fall in love. I could fall in love right here." She shifted on the seat to look at him straight on.

He studied her face. Her bright blue eyes were earnest, but she must be wearing rose-colored contact lenses if she thought he was worthy of her affection.

"Sure. Fall in love here. But it won't be with me. I'm too old for you. I'm too road-worn. Hardened. I'm not suitable husband material. Believe me, I know."

She tilted her head. "You've been married? But not to the baby's mom?"

"Correct. Married once. It didn't work out. Next." No need to tell her about Suze and the brief time of their marriage.

"You're wiser. Experienced. Doesn't make you unlovable."

"It does."

She reached for her beverage, shaking her head. "No. I don't agree. I think if you were with the right woman, you would change your mind."

"And you think you're the right one?"

"Try me. Let's see."

He laughed and looked away. She was ridiculous, but persistent; had to give her props for that. "Time to take you home."

She groaned. "Are you not going to ask me out on a proper date?"

"No."

"Come on. I dare you."

She scooted closer to him on the couch, her knee grazing his hip. He caught a hint of her perfume, something musky and warm. That surprised him; he would have expected her to choose a sickly floral scent.

He wanted to reach behind her head, pull her close and lay a passionate kiss on her lips. Just once, so he could break the hold she had on him.

A date? She was just enthralled with the bad-boy image he portrayed. She wouldn't pursue him like this if she was at home, in her element, with a risk they could run into her friends, family, or even acquaintances. Here, hundreds of miles from home, he was just a potential conquest. A memory she could share with her girlfriends, have a good laugh. Maybe even boost her social status. *Yeah, I dated a dirty biker bartender one time. He was a good time but not a long time.*

He shook his head. This was not a good idea. She was going to break his heart; he knew it. But something inside him wanted her to stay longer. Being around her was easing the stress and guilt he felt about Eva Lyn's impending arrival. "Fine. Would you care to go to dinner with me tomorrow night? It's my only open night before Eva Lyn arrives."

"Yes!" she punctuated the word with a bounce. "I would very much like to go to dinner with you. Now, that wasn't so bad, was it?"

He shook his head. Asking wasn't the hard part. The hard part would be the absence she was going to leave in his life when she left.

Chapter 11

The lanky server set the plate of calamari between them. Quincy scrunched his nose as Sorcha said, "Yum!"

"Not a fan." Quincy reached for his bottle of beer. "You go ahead."

"You're missing out." Grabbing a fork, she raised her eyebrows at him. "Are you sure you don't want any?"

"It's all yours."

"If I had known you wouldn't eat it, I would have passed on the appetizer."

"I'm saving room for the rib eye."

"Do you eat seafood?" She took a bite as they looked towards the Gulf. Clouds blocked the setting sun, but suddenly a burst of pink, orange, and purple streaks broke through, to give them another spectacular view.

They'd driven twenty miles south along the coast to this place. Since it was late, Quincy opted to drive his new-to-him sedan instead of the motorcycle, to Sorcha's disappointment.

Regardless of how they got there, she was thankful for this date. With Quincy picking up all the shifts he could before his daughter arrived, this had been the only available time. *At least I consider it a date; Quincy might just consider it dinner.*

After a pause, Quincy said, "Sure. I eat fish. The other stuff doesn't agree with me."

"So, you have a sensitive stomach. Good to know."

"The *only* sensitive thing about me."

Sorcha shook her head. "I doubt that. I bet you have a soft spot in your heart for sappy movies."

"Does *Dirty Harry* count?"

"Wouldn't know." She shrugged. *Isn't that an old man's movie?* "Haven't seen it."

"Really? We might have to remedy that." If she could get Quincy to watch movies with her, this could lead to something. "I'm game. Do you own it?"

He raised an eyebrow.

"Oh, right." She stabbed at another piece of squid. "You own nothing besides baby stuff and a few articles of clothing. You can travel light."

"Not so light anymore. But now I have a *car*." He drew out the word, like it was disgusting.

"Next thing you know, you're going to have a three-bedroom home, a white picket fence, and books!"

"I have a library card. I don't need to own books."

"There will be some books worth keeping. Reference books. Poetry books. And now, children's books! You're going to have lots of those!"

"Yes to the kid's books. But I'll stop you there. I won't be reading poetry books."

"No? Making a mental note. Now I know what to buy for Christmas."

Quincy let out a huff and shook his head.

The restaurant had few patrons, not too surprising for nine o'clock on a Monday night. "Pretty cool place," Sorcha said, glancing around.

"A lady at work recommended it," Quincy said.

"Jasmyn?"

He shook his head. "No. Tania."

"Have you been here before?" Sorcha asked, taking another bite of calamari.

"No. Never had a desire to before."

When he said "desire", staring at her with his stormy blue eyes, she felt a thrill zip through her body. She smiled when his eyes widened, as if the word had escaped unwittingly out of his mouth.

She hoped that meant he felt some desire for her.

He took a sip of his beer. "You won't remember me by Christmas."

"I wish you'd stop talking like that." She flung up her arms, exasperated, and a small piece of calamari flew off her fork. Reaching to the side, she picked it up with an extra napkin before continuing. "You're always talking about endings. Let's stay focused on the beginning."

"I'm trying to ensure expectations are properly set. I've told you; relationships don't work out for men like me."

"That's just a story you tell yourself. I don't buy it." Having had enough squid (and not wanting to fling more around during the conversation), she put down her fork and set aside the plate.

"If you knew my history, you'd buy it."

"Well, tell me, then. Enlighten me."

Quincy shook his head and leaned forward. "You're not ready for my horror stories."

"I'm calling your bluff right now. We all have horror stories about dating. I'm sure we could go back and forth, one-upping each other."

"Do you have a failed marriage, where you were informed it was over by text message, in your list of horror stories?" He'd mentioned the divorce before but hadn't shared details. Would this story reveal something about him that would deter her interest? This could be interesting.

"A text message?" She leaned forward. "That's harsh. Tell me more."

"I can't say I was completely surprised. Things had been tense for a while, but I thought it was just relationship growing pains. We'd been married just over a year, barely out of the honeymoon phase, when she decided she was done."

"Wow. She didn't talk to you about it? Try to make things better?"

"No. She was done, and that was that. I should have known. I should have seen it coming."

"Harsh."

"See? I'm not marriage material."

"That doesn't mean any such thing. It just means..." She paused and looked towards the water. How could she say this without sounding conceited? "You haven't found the right woman. Someone who understands you. Who can communicate her wants and needs, and who can anticipate your needs."

He grunted. "Someone like you?"

"Maybe."

"I told you. Me and marriage don't mix."

"How many times have you been married?"

"Just the once. It was enough."

"If you'd said you'd been married six or seven times, then maybe I'd agree with your assessment. But once? You're just a little gun-shy. Besides, relationships take two people. Maybe the problem was all on your ex-wife. She didn't tell you what was wrong, so you couldn't fix it. She didn't try to work things out."

Quincy kept shaking his head no, like he wasn't listening. She hoped her words were getting through his thick skull. "Quincy! She didn't fight for you!"

He raised an eyebrow. He'd heard that. "I'm not worth fighting for. She got it right."

Sorcha let out a huff. "You are determined to believe the worst about yourself, aren't you?"

"As I should."

"Hear me out. How many single men do you think would have turned their lives upside down when they heard they had a daughter who needed a home? Hmm? Most wouldn't. But here you've been busting your butt to get ready to take her in, buying everything she needs, asking for help, which I know you can't stand to do." He looked mildly chagrined, so she continued. "Taking extra shifts before she comes. That's really admirable."

Quincy didn't respond. He turned his head to look out at the Gulf, but she could read the embarrassment on his face.

"Most women would be thrilled to be married to a man who did that. The others are idiots." Sorcha felt her face grow hot. She was on a soapbox again, speaking her opinion. This is when most men she dated realized she was too much. Too opinionated. Too hard to control.

"And how often have you been married, young lady?"

Young lady? That sent a bristle down her back. "I haven't. Yet. Maybe I won't be. Guys don't seem to consider me marriage material."

"What?" Quincy cried, turning back towards her.

She twirled the thin silver bangle bracelet around her wrist. It had been a gift from her mom when she graduated high school.

How much did she want to share with Quincy? Maybe telling him about her long string of failed relationships would turn him off.

"It's true," she said. "Men see me as the party girl. The one you date, not the one you take home to your mom or propose to. Or they get turned off when they figure out that I have opinions." She sighed.

This was harder than she'd expected. She usually brushed these thoughts aside, never lingering on them. If a girlfriend asked how her dating life was going, she'd brush it off, putting on the air of someone who wasn't looking to settle down. *Love 'em and leave 'em, I always say.* She looked down at her hands, arms crossed, and resting on the table.

Quincy reached across, gently grasping her forearm. "Hey. You are too harsh on yourself. I bet men are just intimidated by your beauty and charm. They probably get tongue-tied around you and feel like prepubescent boys. One of these days, you are going to find a confident, successful man who sees your worth and will fall all over himself to win you over. Be patient."

His touch warmed her; she'd longed for the heat of his skin on hers.

"Besides," he continued. "I like your opinions. Keep 'em."

Maybe her problem was dating the upwardly-mobile types. The dudes that hung out in big clusters, shouting at the game on the big screen. Up to this point, they'd seemed like the ones she should want. Handsome, outgoing, with important jobs. Wealthy. Fine, upstanding citizens.

But looking at Quincy, with his tattoos, dark clothes, and stay-away attitude, she realized he had the qualities she'd been missing; mystery, integrity, a willingness to fight for what was right, like taking responsibility for a baby he hadn't known he had.

Would the other guys she'd dated do that? Or would they just offer to pay money to make the problem go away?

She was always encouraging and fighting for others. It was sad to realize that no guy had ever done that for her.

She shifted in her chair. "I'm always fighting for someone else. Telling them to dream bigger, ask for the raise, speak up for themselves, voice their opinion. But no man ever does that for me."

The waiter placed their dinners in front of them. Sorcha appreciated the distraction. This conversation wasn't about her; it was about Quincy. She wanted to get him to see himself differently. As someone deserving of love.

She thought about his daughter. She wanted the little girl to be raised by a self-confident man with a positive attitude towards relationships. The road ahead was going to be tough for the little girl. It was tough for kids with two emotionally strong parents. She might not be a parent, but she knew that much from teaching third grade for years.

Sorcha took a deep breath. Her path was clear. By the time she left Florida, Quincy was going to shed this doubt about his lovability.

Once Quincy had dropped Sorcha off, he took a slow drive along the roads of Seaside Bay and the surrounding county, drifting aimlessly through one small, lazy beach town after another.

He needed the time to clear his head. He drove with the windows down and no radio playing, listening to the sounds of night birds, traffic, and occasional music from a passing car.

It was official; his life had now turned completely around. Just two weeks ago, Sorcha had blown in on the wind like Dorothy landing in the Land of Oz. A pretty girl with sparkling shoes and a stunning personality.

And then to find out he had a daughter! Mind blowing.

If anyone had told him all this a few weeks ago, he would have laughed in their face and driven off on his motorcycle. Now, he was driving around in a sedan contemplating a beautiful blonde and his soon-to-be-seen little girl with "the prettiest blue eyes".

He wished he'd thought of asking Ms. Myer for a picture; she could have sent one. But in a way, not having one made the anticipation even more exciting.

Slowing for a stop sign, he glanced at a pretty, bright blue house on the corner. He stayed for a few seconds, as there was no one behind him, and sat gazing at the little bungalow-style home with the white fence.

He daydreamed about sitting on the front step, watching his daughter play on the well-manicured lawn, listening to someone in the kitchen preparing dinner and singing. Sorcha?

Shaking his head, he put his foot on the accelerator. Sorcha's comments about his ex-wife may have had him questioning his assumptions about himself, but he wasn't ready to consider a future with her.

But her comment about someone fighting for him? That had turned his gut inside out. It made him look at her differently. She was a fighter. He could imagine her going to the mat against the school board or an unruly parent if she felt one of her students was being mistreated. She said others called her too opinionated, but society needed more disrupters fighting for the underdog. He liked that about her. *Really* liked that about her. Another way he differed from the young men in her crowd.

For the first time, he didn't think that was a bad thing.

Chapter 12

Thankful that Linda's family allowed her to drive their car, Sorcha set off for a day of shopping, stopping first at The Coastal Drip, where she bought an extra-large iced vanilla latte to fuel her shopping adventure. She usually preferred hot coffee, but the Florida heat had her ordering iced.

Her first stop was at Second Time's the Charm, a cute resale boutique about five miles from the beach. She had to remind herself several times that she wasn't shopping for her own clothes as she meandered around the store. She loved searching for bright beach clothes while she was in Florida; the selection was better than she ever found in Illinois.

The shopping cart had one wonky wheel, but that didn't stop her from finagling it up and down the aisles of baby clothes. For a thrift shop in an area that skewed to an older demographic, the volume and variety of baby clothes shocked her.

She checked each item for stains and wear, excited to see that quite a few clothes still had their original tags. That detail reminded her that babies grow fast, so she tempered the urge to throw every cute piece of clothing into the cart.

Leaving the store with two large bags full of clothes, she walked towards the car while searching on her phone for the next thrift store. The screen alerted her to an incoming call from Linda, and she paused on the sidewalk to answer it.

"Hey, Lulu! What's up?" She stepped out of the way of an older gentleman walking an energetic poodle. They wore matching sun visors, which made Sorcha smile.

"Taking a break, and wanted to check in. What are you up to today?"

Sorcha hadn't talked to Linda since she'd found out about Quincy's baby. This might be a marathon conversation.

"How much time do you have?" she asked.

Linda laughed. "You're supposed to be on vacation. How can you have a lot to tell me? You're supposed to be tanning, eating, and drinking. Um..." She paused, and Sorcha started walking to the car. "I can chat for approximately twenty minutes, unless a customer walks in."

Linda ran her own stationery boutique.

"That should work. Hold on a sec, I'm putting bags in the car." She fiddled with the trunk, dropped the bags in, and got into the car. Starting the car to get the air conditioner running, she continued, "Well, I am out shopping today, but not for myself."

"Yeah?" Linda sounded curious and a little alarmed.

"Remember Quincy from Crabbie's?"

"Of course. Tell me he's fallen under your spell, and you're out shopping to make him a romantic dinner."

"I wish. No, this is not that. Though, maybe over time that's the bigger egg to crack...never mind. No, bigger than that."

"Oh, gosh. What in the world? Tell me!"

Sorcha took a breath. "He has a baby. He was just told about her, and she's coming to live with him. Her mom died."

"Get out! That's big. Sounds like he's got a lot going on. Probably not an egg you should try to crack. What are you shopping for?"

"Baby clothes. She arrives on Thursday, and he has nothing. We shopped on Sunday for most of the supplies: crib, stroller, baby stuff, foodstuff, but we ran out of time to get clothes."

"Won't she arrive with clothes?"

"Sure. Probably. But I'm still shopping. I'm thrifting, so not like it will cost a lot." She thought of the seventy dollars she'd already spent.

"Can you return the items if they're not needed?"

"Not sure. But I can donate them. Either back to the thrift store or I could take them to a women and children's emergency shelter."

"Well. Forget the clothes for a minute. What does this mean for Quincy? How's he going to manage? Wait. He didn't ask you to marry him and take care of his baby, did he?"

"Don't be ridiculous." Though the thought had crossed her mind, Sorcha would not tell Linda. It sounded too irrational. "No, I'm just helping him out. Getting prepared. But..." She paused. Things were happening so fast. "I wanted to see if I could stay two more weeks in the condo. He needs a sitter or nanny, and I'm going to help him interview for one, but in the meantime, I told him I could babysit until he hires someone permanently. If someone else is coming to your family's place, that's fine. I could look for a rental or maybe even stay at Quincy's. His place is small, but he has a couch."

"*You'd* sleep on a *couch* for this guy?"

"Sure. Why not?"

"Sor', careful. It sounds like a tricky situation. You could be an easy mark for him. He never seemed like a father figure to me. He may end up dumping the baby on you. Did you think about that?"

"That's outrageous. He wouldn't do that. You don't know him."

"And you don't, either. Not really. At most, you have a crush on this guy. He's hot. I get why you're enamored with him. But don't fall into something you can't dig your way out of."

Sorcha's ears burned. The A/C was not doing its job. She turned the knob to a higher fan setting. Her heart started pounding, and she felt her pulse in her big toe. Not good.

"It's fine, Linda. I've spent some time with him outside of the bar, getting to know him. He's quiet, reserved, but he's more interested in not getting hurt and doing the right thing than you might suspect."

Linda sighed deeply. "Look, I'm not trying to throw cold water over you. I just know you've been crushing on this guy since we first saw him last year. Throw a baby who's lost her mama into the mix, and the threats to your heart are real. Just protect yourself. I'll ask about the condo. My family is flying down on July second for the wedding, but I don't know if Uncle Paul is planning to be there, or whether he has other guests coming. I'll find out."

"Thank you, I appreciate it. And I hear what you're saying, but I feel good about this. I want to help him. It won't lead to anything long term. I have to go back to reality at some point. Probably back to teaching."

"Have you made any progress on the job search?"

"Not in the last few days; I've been helping Quincy. But when I get back to the condo today, I'll work on it."

"OK. I'll let you know about extending your stay as soon as I can."

"Thanks. Not to change the subject, but how are wedding plans coming along? Anything I can help with from here?"

"We're in good shape. But if you could check with Meridian, the building manager, and make sure she saw my email about packages arriving there this week and next, I would appreciate it."

"Certainly, I'd be happy to. I haven't seen much of her since I've been here. I'll stop by her office today."

"Thanks. Good luck shopping."

"Thanks. I'm finding so many cute things. This baby is going to be so stylish."

Linda laughed. "Of course she is. She's got Auntie Sorchie shopping for her. She's in excellent hands. What's the baby's name, by the way?"

"Eva Lyn."

"Awe. Cute. Gotta run. A customer just walked in."

"OK. Talk later."

Sorcha hung up and tossed her phone on the passenger seat. That had not gone as well as she'd hoped. Linda's push-back seemed unfair. Sorcha knew what she was doing. Of course, she should not get caught up in the fantasy of becoming part of Quincy's family. That was ridiculous. This was vacation and not real life. But it was Quincy's real life, and she was happy to help him out while she could.

She needed to get serious about job hunting. She was hoping she'd have some interviews lined up by the end of the month, if she didn't get too distracted by helping Quincy out.

Ideally, she would put in her resignation to the school office before August first, so they could start hunting for a replacement. She didn't want to leave the school or the students in the lurch.

Maybe she could include the Seaside Bay area in her job-search locations. If she found something here, she could arrange her schedule to help Quincy out a little longer. She added 'search for apartments' to her mental to-do list. She had one big change coming up with the career move. Why not add a relocation to the mix? Come to think about it, there wasn't anything holding her in Illinois.

She thought about her dad and his wish for her to buy a house close to his neighborhood. She appreciated the idea, but he'd always told her to do what was right for her. Besides, he was busy with Barb and his stepsons. He would hardly miss her.

Go big or go home.

She picked up her phone again, searching for the next thrift store, and started the map directions on the GPS. These baby clothes would not buy themselves.

The next day, Sorcha stood in front of the couch, where she'd dumped the laundry basket of freshly washed and dried baby clothes.

She'd left the condo's balcony door open, and a warm breeze rustled the drapes. The briny smell of the Gulf aroused Sorcha's impatience. She wanted to get to the pool while it was still in the sunshine. In a couple of hours, the building would block the sun, and she'd move to the beach to continue tanning. After she'd thrown the last load into the dryer, she'd pulled on her bikini and a loose cover-up that fell just below her hips.

Folding a pink T-shirt with Minnie Mouse on it, Sorcha smiled. She couldn't wait to take the clothes to Quincy's and put them away in the small white dresser she'd found while thrift shopping the day before.

Quincy was working his third double shift today. She hoped these extra-long workdays weren't sapping all his energy. He was going to need it when Eva Lyn arrived. He was so busy that she didn't know when she'd be able to drop the baby clothes off, but at least she would be ready when he told her she could.

Linda had called the night before and confirmed that Sorcha could stay in the condo for two more weeks. No one was planning to stay there until July. Thrilled, she'd texted Quincy right away to tell him the good news, and his relief was clear in the three exclamation marks he'd sent back. He asked if she could babysit five days the following week, and she agreed.

All morning, while washing baby clothes and blankets, Sorcha had searched countless mom blogs for advice on raising toddlers: ideas for food, for entertaining them, getting them to sleep, and even using sign language. Her research taught her that eighteen-month-olds could even have some verbal skills, but there was no telling how a child who'd lost her mom and spent time in foster care would be coping emotionally.

Sorcha had put on a calm and confident persona with Quincy, but she wasn't all that confident handling a baby. Her kid experience was mainly with seven and eight-year-olds. She thought about calling her stepmom for advice, but didn't want to share too much too soon.

Placing the last article of clothing into the basket, Sorcha tossed some poolside items into her tote bag: sunscreen, a towel, sunglasses, and a couple of magazines.

Once she had everything she needed, she shut the balcony door, turned on the air-conditioning, and slid into her flip-flops.

When she got off the elevator on the first floor, she walked to Meridian's office and knocked lightly.

"Come in!" came the woman's voice from inside the office.

"Hi," Sorcha said, pushing the door open. "Not sure if you remember me. I'm Sorcha. Staying in the Brees family's condo. I'm friends with Linda.

"Oh, right." Meridian pulled out a basket of mini chocolate bars. "Want one?" When Sorcha shook her head, she took one for herself. "What can I do for you?"

"Linda asked me to stop by. She said she emailed you, but she wanted to make sure you know that she'll have several boxes shipped here before the wedding."

"Right-o. I saw it. Guess I should email her back. Not a problem; I'll put them in the locked storage room. They'll be fine. Are you staying until the wedding? It's in two weeks, right?

"Um, more like three and a half. It's on July fifth. I'll be here for the wedding, but I'm not staying the whole time. I'll fly home for a few days beforehand. We have a girls' spa day planned, and I have to get my dress from the tailor. I'd like to stay, but I'm looking forward to being home with my roommate before she gets married."

"That's nice. You enjoying your visit?"

"Yes. Always."

"Just you?"

"Yes."

"Well, if you get bored or lonely, let me know. I can usually find something to keep you busy." The woman's eyes sparkled. She was a mischievous one.

"I'm going to be helping a friend out, so I don't expect to be bored, but I'll let you know. I won't keep you. Heading to the pool for a while before I move to the beach."

"All righty. Enjoy yourself! Candy for the road?" She held up the basket again.

"No, that's OK. Thank you!"

Sorcha ran into Winnie and Rosalie in the hallway. They were on their way to the pool as well.

"Great to see you ladies," Sorcha said.

"Hey, it's that pretty Yankee!" Winnie said.

Rosalie stopped. "Hi, hon. Coming to keep us company?"

"Yes, absolutely."

Outside, they pulled three lounge chairs into the sunshine. Sorcha was glad to see that these ladies weren't interested in the shade, either.

Settled, Winnie opened a small red cooler covered in stickers, all featuring bands, by the looks of it; Sorcha could make out Eagles and Rolling Stones stickers.

"Do you like live music, Winnie?" she asked.

"Oh, yes. There was nothing better than going to a concert. I especially love going to the three-day festivals. Pitching a tent, wandering around campsites, talking to strangers. Buying unique wares from artisan vendors. It's a hoot! My poor back can't tolerate sleeping in a tent anymore, so I stick to the festivals with motels close by."

"I can see you rocking the fest," Sorcha said as she slathered sunscreen over her legs. She loved to work on the tan, but with her blond hair and fair skin, it took a lot of time and a lot of caution.

Rosalie took out a magazine and began flipping through the pages. Sorcha glanced over to see it was an AARP magazine with Martin Sheen on the cover. "Yeah, back in the day, Winnie would wander into her share of tents, looking for love."

Sorcha coughed and choked at the same time. "Really? Winnie, I thought you were the quiet one."

"It's the quiet ones that ya gotta worry about," Winnie retorted, opening a small cooler and pulling out a light beer.

"True story." Sorcha adjusted her large straw hat and lay back to catch some rays. This was heaven. She was thankful she was going to stay in Florida for two more weeks, but knew she wouldn't get a lot of extra sun time while watching Quincy's daughter.

"So, have you hooked up with the hunky bartender yet?" Winnie asked, taking a long sip of her beer.

"Not looking for a hook-up..."

"Yeah, right."

"Winnie, shut up. Leave the gal alone. Go on, hon." Rosalie motioned for a beverage and Winnie grabbed some water for her from the cooler.

Sorcha shook her head. *These two are a trip!* "I would like to get to know him better and date him, but his life is getting much more complicated. He just found out he has a little girl, and he's getting custody. He asked if I could help watch her until he gets a permanent nanny. Luckily, I could extend my stay to help."

"What? A daughter?" Winnie snorted. "By the looks of him, I bet that man has a dozen. He gets hit on more often than a boxer in a prize fight going twelve rounds."

"I hope not," Sorcha replied. "He seems pretty freaked out about just one child."

"Can't imagine it will be easy on him. He needs a good woman. The babe needs a mama. Where's her mama?"

"She died."

Both women gasped. "Oh, no," Rosalie said. "That's just awful. But you said he just found out. How old's the poor thing? Why didn't he know about her before?"

"I don't know all the details and don't mean to gossip."

"It's not gossip. It's storytelling. Learn the difference," Winnie said.

"I'd like to see the different definitions."

"Never mind that. Go on. Tell us what you know."

"That's about it. The baby is around eighteen months old. It's going to be hard, isn't it? She doesn't know Quincy, and she might be frightened."

"He is a little gruff-looking. That beard and all those tattoos." Rosalie tossed her magazine down.

"I'm sure she'll get used to him quickly, dear." Winnie leaned forward with a big smile. "My grandson Tristan is covered in tattoos, but his kids adore him. It's more about how you treat them than how you look."

"You're right. I'm sure they'll bond quick enough."

Sorcha thought about the challenge ahead, but she was confident Quincy would succeed. He was the quiet, determined type of person. All action, little talk. He probably didn't need forty-seven conversations about looking for a new job. He probably just plowed ahead until he was successful at getting one.

She could learn a thing or two from Quincy. Like how to be the strong, silent type, rather than the 'talking to everyone about everything half a dozen times before taking action' type. Like with job hunting. She had the desire but hadn't put forth enough effort. That was changing today. Once she finished tanning for the day, she'd log into the three different job sites she'd signed up for and start applying. She'd throw as many darts out as it took to find something new.

Maybe she could even find a remote job and stay on in Florida indefinitely helping Quincy. Not to get ahead of herself, but the idea was too intriguing to ignore. Rosalie and Winnie started talking about where they were going to dinner. Sorcha took out her phone to text Quincy.

> **Sorcha**: How's it going?

After a few seconds, he replied.

> **Quincy:** Getting ready to head to work. You gonna stop by tonight?

Well, she couldn't job hunt *all* night.

> **Sorcha:** Yes, I thought I could grab the key to your place and drop off the stuff I washed, so it's there when Eva arrives tomorrow.

She watched the three dots appear and disappear. Was she being too forward? She could tell he liked his personal space, but still.

> **Quincy:** Sorry. Customer. Yeah, that would be great. Thanks again.

Whew. Good reminder not to jump to conclusions.

Chapter 13

Quincy paced between the leather couch and the front door countless times, checking the clock that hung on the wall. It had come with the house. It wasn't one Quincy would choose; the face was a pink and blue gingham pattern that reminded him of something his grandmother would have had back in the eighties.

Waiting was unbearable. He should have left some important tasks for this morning, like putting together the highchair or the crib. Anything to fill his mind and busy his hands.

He'd picked up every extra shift he could for the last two weeks so he could afford to take time off when Eva Lyn arrived. Even with the extra hours on the job and the extra tasks involved in preparing his home for the little girl, he had plenty of time to worry.

Although he'd originally asked Sorcha to be there when Eva Lyn and Ms. Myer arrived, upon further deliberation he changed his mind. He needed to do this alone. It would be alarming enough for the kid to come to a new house and be left with a strange, ugly man. Having Sorcha there too would only have added to the poor kid's stress.

At the sound of an approaching car, Quincy yanked the door open and stepped onto the porch. A light blue sedan pulled closer and parked.

Taking a deep breath, he forced himself not to run down the sidewalk. He counted his footsteps as he approached the car.

The car's trunk popped open, then a woman got out of the driver's side and regarded Quincy. "Mr. Halford?" she asked.

"That's me. Ms. Myer?"

She smiled, weary but pleased. "Yes. I'll get Eva Lyn. Will you grab the two bags in the trunk?"

He nodded and walked to the back of the car.

Passing the back window, he looked in to see the sleeping child and stopped short.

If someone had told him his heart would squeeze upon seeing the face of his child, he would have launched into a heated argument about how ridiculous the statement was. But now? The squeezing started in his heart and quickly spread through every muscle in his body.

I'm not ready for this.

Ms. Myer approached him from the left; he hadn't heard her coming but felt her presence. Realizing that he was blocking her from getting Eva Lyn, he proceeded to the trunk and grabbed the bags he found there. "Both cases are the baby's?" he asked. Ms. Myer nodded, and he led the way inside, glancing around to assure himself that the yard and porch were still tidy. They must be. Unable to sleep last night, he'd spent hours cleaning the small home until it practically sparkled.

Would Ms. Myer find him suitable to take charge of a baby? Since it was a warm night, he was wearing a loose, long-sleeved T-shirt to cover his tattoos. He'd even considered shaving his beard, but thought the gesture would be overly dramatic. The tan line created by removing his beard would look ridiculous for a while, and rather than incurring the ridicule of his co-workers because of his baby face, he decided against it.

In the living room, the social worker set the baby seat on the floor and looked around, checking out the room.

"Can I get you something to drink?" he asked.

"Not yet, but I could use the bathroom."

"Of course. It's the door on the left." He pointed to the door and Ms. Myer put her bags on the couch and left the room.

Quincy took a deep breath and approached the baby seat. Eva Lyn was still sleeping.

"Long drive, huh, kid?" he asked as he sat down and scooted the seat closer to the couch.

The movement caused the little girl to squirm and open one eye, but she quickly closed it again and sighed.

He wanted to take her out of the contraption but worried she'd be cranky if he woke her. He settled for unsnapping the buckles.

His knuckles felt the slightly damp material of her shirt. He studied her from head to toe, noting the soft curls in her blonde hair, the fullness of her cheeks, and her adorable pursed lips.

She wore a light pink T-shirt with the words "Daddy's Girl," in a bold, purple font, a pair of purple cotton pants, and white sandals.

He wondered if she was hot in the long pants. He ran an uncertain hand over her head; she didn't feel too warm.

The bathroom door opened and he glanced over his shoulder. "Care for some water or a soda now?"

"Water would be great." The social worker walked to the couch where her bags were but didn't sit down. She put her hands on her hips and swayed side to side. "I've had two sixty-four-ounce diet sodas already today. I'm not a fan of long road trips."

Quincy walked to the refrigerator in the kitchen area—it was an open-concept space before open-concept was cool—and grabbed two bottles of water.

"I appreciate you making this one, then," he said.

She took the water from him, opened it, and gulped down half the bottle. "I needed that," she said. "Glad she's still asleep. It will give us time to go over some paperwork.

Her last foster family put together a very detailed list of important information: which foods she likes and doesn't like, her eating and sleeping schedules, and some watch points."

"Watch points?"

"She's dealing with the loss of her mother. Being so young, we sometimes think such things can't affect them, but they do. In the last two months, she's been shuffled in and out of three foster homes. Luckily, she was in the last one for a month, so they could take the time to get to know her and bring her some stability." Ms. Myer paused and fished in her bag for a couple of folders, one of which she handed to Quincy.

"Here are the notes from the family," she continued. "The schedule is on top, followed by food preferences and general notes. Traveling today has thrown the schedule off. She will probably stay up later than eight o'clock tonight. Give her a day or two to adjust, and she should be back on schedule."

"Ms. Myer?"

She turned to look at him. "Hmm?"

"Are you really going to leave her with me with just a few pages of notes?"

She gave him a half-smile. "I am. As soon as I confirm your identity. I'll need your driver's license, by the way, and I'll look over the place to ensure you have a proper setup to take care of her. Normal procedures, don't worry."

"Thanks for the list you provided. I think we have everything."

"We?" She raised her eyebrows. "I thought you were single."

Quincy nodded. "I am. A friend helped me shop."

"Worried you were in over your head?"

"Something like that."

She took out a notepad and pen. "You'll be fine, Mr. Halford. The fact that you cared enough to ask for help will serve you well. Can I look around?"

"Sure."

Ms. Myer left the room, and the baby stirred. She sighed, smacked her lips, and opened one eye slowly, then the other. She blinked at Quincy with furrowed brows.

"Hi, Eva Lyn. I'm your dad. Nice to meet you." He took her tiny hand in his, amazed at the softness of her skin, and gently pumped her hand up and down in a formal handshake. "I'm gonna be upfront with you; I don't know what I'm doing. But I'm going to give it my all. You can count on me."

Eva Lyn shifted her head from one side of her carrier to the other, as though she was assessing his words, taking stock. Quincy wasn't sure if he was getting his point across when her lips trembled. She closed her eyes and wailed.

"Fuuu...mpkin." Quincy twisted around. Ms. Myer had gone into the bedroom. Would she come and rescue him?

If the social worker heard the baby's cries, she wasn't running back to help. Maybe this was a test.

It had been several years since his niece and nephew were this little, but he thought he remembered the basics. He placed his hands under her arms and lifted her out of the carrier, bringing her to his chest. The change of location seemed to appease her for a moment. Her crying stopped as she looked around the room.

Quincy carefully leaned over and picked up the pages of notes—listing food suggestions, necessary vaccinations by age, and some developmental and behavioral milestones.

Scanning the food list, he was relieved to see that Eva could drink whole milk. He had some in the fridge, so he poured it into a freshly washed bottle.

In a quiet voice, he gave Eva Lyn a play-by-play of all his actions. She peered at him, if not with trust per se, at least with cautious optimism.

"You and me both," he said, lifting the bottle towards her mouth. She reached out with her impossibly small hands and took it from him.

"A self-starter. I like that." Quincy walked toward the sink and pointed out the window to the trees behind his small house. After a few seconds, a colorful bird flew onto the top of the outdoor storage shed that housed the lawnmower.

Eva Lyn let out a small gasp and looked at him with large eyes.

"Did you see the bird?" Quincy asked her. Her eyes were the same shade of bright blue as his. He shook his head. *Don't think we need a DNA test. Everyone in my mom's line has those blue eyes.*

Ms. Myer came out of the bedroom. "She's awake." She walked closer. "Hi there, honey. Got some milk?"

Eva giggled, and the shaking of her body eased the tension in Quincy's shoulders. *Giggling has to be good. Hope she doesn't have a meltdown when Ms. Myer leaves.*

"Mind if I look in the fridge and cabinets?"

"Go ahead."

Quincy had bought five of every item on the food list that Ms. Myer had emailed him. He feared running out of something crucial when the stores were closed.

Jotting notes on her paper and murmuring to herself, Ms. Myer went about the kitchen. Quincy walked Eva Lyn towards the front door, pointing out the furniture and pictures on the wall, none of which actually belonged to him. She seemed to enjoy listening and looking. He hoped that meant she'd settle into her new life soon. The transition was going to be painful, no matter how much attention he gave to it. His daughter had lost her mother and been in foster care. She didn't even know him, but he knew he had to do the right thing and raise her. It wouldn't be easy for either of them, but he would figure it out. He had to.

Once the social worker had made her observations about his home, they sat down to talk.

"Things appear to be in order," she said, skimming her checklist. "I would prefer a two-bedroom house, but you haven't had enough time to pull that off. I like how you hung the drapes to section off her area of the bedroom. Here." She handed him a piece of paper, retaining a carbon copy for herself. "This is a list of a few hazards that need to be addressed right away. Tipping hazards, cabinet locks, etc. Complete this list as quickly as you can. I'm working with a local social worker, who will follow up in a few days."

"All right. I'll tackle this right away."

"Good. Well, I'm sure you have more questions for me." She turned her clipboard sideways, setting it on her legs and pulling it towards herself. "Though I daresay you've asked a lot already." She gave him a wide grin, showing she was teasing.

"I've got most of them out of the way. But I wanted to ask about Leeza. Do you know any more about the cause of death?"

"You should call the coroner's office and get the official report, but as you assumed, it was an apparent overdose. I don't believe toxicology is complete yet. It will provide a final analysis."

"That's terrible. I wish I had stayed and done more to help her."

"Don't beat yourself up. Sometimes we have to remove ourselves from situations for our own good. From a few conversations I had with her neighbors, it seems Ms. Shelton got clean once she realized she was pregnant. From everything I heard, she remained clean until recently. It might have been her first and only relapse that killed her."

Wow. She cleaned up when she knew she was pregnant, probably not long after I left. Would things have turned out all right if he'd stayed?

Ms. Myer flipped through the papers on her clipboard, found the one she was looking for, and handed it to him. "Here, these are the names and phone numbers of everyone I spoke to. They may give you some more answers about Ms. Shelton and her daughter, fill in some gaps."

He had enough on his plate right now getting Eva Lyn settled, but maybe someday in the future he would make a phone call or two. "Thank you for this list."

An hour later, Ms. Myer had finished what she needed to accomplish. They moved the car seat foundation from her car to his, and she said her goodbyes.

Watching her pull away from the curb, Eva Lyn began to cry, just as Quincy had feared. Hoping for the best, he took her inside and showed her the lights and sounds made by the electronic baby book he'd bought. Soon, she was pushing buttons and giggling, all thoughts of Ms. Myer gone.

"It's you and me, Evie. It's gonna be a rough and rocky start, but we'll get through it."

Sorcha put down the crochet hooks and picked up her phone for the tenth time. The social worker should have dropped off Quincy's daughter *hours* ago.

He hadn't said he'd call or text her afterwards, but Sorcha had hoped he would.

She consulted the crochet pattern again and started a new row of stitches.

Concentrating, she chewed on her lower lip. This was the first time she'd attempted to make a crocheted animal, but when she saw the pattern for the stuffed cat, she knew she had to try it. It would be an adorable gift for Quincy's daughter, as long as it didn't end up with three ears or five legs.

She desperately wanted to know how it was going. She couldn't imagine the responsibility of being handed a toddler for the first time and hearing the words, "Here you go. Good luck."

Did he get any instructions? Is he freaking out?

Sorcha thought about calling Linda and venting about not hearing from Quincy, but Linda had so much on her mind with her upcoming wedding, it would be selfish to bother her.

The television was on a game show channel. She'd seen three episodes of *The Price is Right* and two of *Family Feud*. After hours of shopping for Quincy's daughter, she thought she could ace an appearance in any pricing competition.

"Oh! I can't take it anymore!" She tossed the yarn and needles down and grabbed her phone again.

> **Sorcha**: How's it going? Can you talk?

She knew he might just text, but she muted the TV, anyway. With any luck, Quincy would just call her. Alas, a minute later, her phone chirped.

> **Quincy**: Give me ten minutes. Need a shower. Will call.

Sorcha imagined Quincy getting in and out of the shower. She fanned herself, thinking about Quincy in nothing but a towel, rivulets of water traveling over his chest and tattoos. She knew all about the tattoos covering his arms and neck, as she'd studied them countless times while sitting at the bar. But she didn't know if there were any on his chest, back, or legs. At the refrigerator, she grabbed a cold Pepsi, and walked out onto the balcony to get a view of the Gulf.

The sun had set, but the horizon still displayed streaks of pink and purple. Stars were out, and she sat in a chair, admiring the view.

Wishing she was strolling the beach with Quincy, she took a sip of the soda and closed her eyes.

Stop it. Even if he was interested, he doesn't have time for a relationship right now. If he doesn't have a sitter and is asking me to help, how are we going to go on a date? We couldn't.

She listed all the reasons it wouldn't work. They lived in separate states. He had a kid to take care of; there would be no whirlwind romance, no wining and dining. *I can't get attached to a little kid whose dad hasn't shown any interest in me and who may pick up and move with little to no notice.*

If she got attached, it would be too painful if things didn't work out between her and Quincy. Not only would she and Quincy be damaged, but she couldn't let his child get hurt if things went south.

Her stepmother hadn't come into her life until she was in her twenties, but it was still difficult. It wasn't that her stepmom was taking her mom's place, but Sorcha still had to go through the adjustment phases when her dad started dating and eventually married Barb. Then there were the stepbrothers. It was complicated. She understood the disruption in Quincy's world, and she didn't want to complicate their lives even more.

Her phone rang, and she picked it up before the first ring had finished.

"Hi," she breathed, trying to sound calm.

"Hey." He sounded exhausted. This would be a quick conversation.

"How was the shower?"

"Much needed. Evie spit up on me."

A loud laugh burst from Sorcha. It took her a moment to recover. "What did you do to her?"

"I don't think she likes peas. It wasn't on her preference sheet."

"She came with a preference sheet?"

"Yeah. Her last foster family took good notes. Guess they hadn't tried peas."

Sorcha chuckled softly. "So how did it go?"

"Good. Pretty painless; a few tears. I had to rock her to sleep. She wouldn't go down on her own."

"See? Told you that you needed the rocking chair."

"It was a great call. What are you doing this evening?"

Interesting. He'd changed the subject pretty fast. Sorcha was expecting a recap of everything he'd done with his daughter, but she wasn't getting one.

"Trying a new craft."

"Yeah?"

"Mm, hmm. Thought I would make something for your baby."

"You don't have to do that. Besides what we bought, she came with a bunch of stuffed animals. The social worker said there were some more things coming, too. Should ship in the next few days."

"When you get ready to move this time, you may actually need a moving truck."

"My days of traveling light are definitely over."

"Well, I shouldn't keep you. I just wanted to make sure you were OK."

"We're good." The tone of his voice didn't match his words. "It's not going to be easy, but we're going to figure it out."

"Let me know how I can help."

"Believe me, I'm calling in that promise. Just give me a few days to get her settled. I don't work until Wednesday."

"All right. Call me tomorrow night; check in."

"I will. Night, Sorcha."

"Good night, Poppa Q."

Quincy chuckled, and it warmed Sorcha's skin. She hung up the call and pressed the soda can to her forehead.

I have to guard my heart. There's no room in Quincy's life for anyone else right now.

Chapter 14

Quincy had asked Sorcha to wait two more days before visiting so he could focus on getting his daughter settled.

Walking up the steps carrying two large tote bags filled with groceries, nervous butterflies danced in her stomach. She'd promised Quincy that she would cook dinner, and he'd sounded relieved. She hoped she wouldn't disappoint him.

She wasn't the best cook, but she could make decent spaghetti with meat sauce and homemade garlic bread. Plus, she'd brought the fixings to make a key lime pie for dessert. She'd asked Quincy for his top five favorite desserts, and he'd said cheesecake and key lime were his favorites. She couldn't remember the others on the list.

Knocking lightly in case the little one was asleep, Sorcha waited on the porch. She turned towards the Gulf, trying to get a view of the water through the trees to help calm her nerves.

When the door clicked open, she whirled around and smiled to see Quincy carrying his little girl.

He seemed relaxed, a natural with the child. He was wearing shorts and a faded New York Knicks T-shirt. She'd never seen him dressed so casually. She glanced down at his legs. No tattoos. Interesting.

The little girl's blue eyes, so much like her daddy's, enchanted Sorcha. Her soft blonde hair reached her shoulders, and her bangs needed a trim. Her cheeks were light pink, like the color of Sorcha's favorite rose.

Eva Lyn eyed Sorcha cautiously. Sorcha wondered for the first time what the girl's mother had looked like. She would ask Quincy later if he had any pictures of his ex on his phone.

The girl was holding a small toy in her hand and extended it towards Sorcha. "Ba," she squeaked.

"Hello," Sorcha said. "Is that a ball? I think it looks more like a car, but that's just me. Ba it is."

The little girl smiled and pulled the toy back.

"Sorcha, this is Evie. Evie, Sorcha. Come in." He pulled the door open wider and Sorcha walked in.

The living room looked chaotic in the best possible way. There was a blanket on the floor with toys scattered across it. A baby doll lay half on, half off the couch. A book stack teetered sideways in the middle of the couch. The small coffee table sat in front of the TV stand, covered with assorted pieces of dollhouse furniture.

Noticing her look at the table, Quincy said, "She loves to stand there and play. Plus, it keeps her away from the TV. I had to secure the stand to the wall. The social worker pointed out the tipping hazard. Also, it gives me some peace knowing she can't get into the doors and drawers."

Sorcha nodded as she walked to the kitchen table, setting down the bags of food. "How hungry are you? I could start dinner now or wait a bit."

"Let's wait. I was thinking we could take a little stroll on the beach, get some fresh air. It seems Evie sleeps better when we have some outdoor time."

"Great! I need to put a few things in the fridge, then I'm good to go."

Quincy put sandals on Evie as Sorcha busied about the kitchen. He asked Sorcha to grab a pail that contained shovels and beach toys, picked up a large beach blanket, and they headed out the door.

As they walked, he told Sorcha about the social worker's visit, the information the foster family had sent with her, and the challenge they'd had getting her sleep schedule worked out. The trick was a small stuffed dog she had to have in her hand to fall asleep. Quincy was thankful that the stuffed animal had come with her.

"Sounds like you're figuring it out. She looks happy," Sorcha said as they spread the blanket on the sand.

"I think she is. She cries for 'mama' when she lies down, but not for long."

"Evie, huh?"

"Yeah. Eva Lyn feels like an old lady's name. Maybe because it was my grandmother's name. She seems to like Evie."

"Did the social worker or the foster family call her Evie?"

"Not sure. Ms. Myer just referred to her as Eva Lyn. And the foster family notes said Eva Lyn. I wonder what her mom called her. If she used Eva Lyn."

"Can you reach out to any of your ex's friends? Would they know?"

"Funny. Great minds." He smiled at her. "The social worker left some names and numbers of Leeza's friends and suggested I call. I'm not ready to do that yet. I'm afraid it will add to my guilt about leaving."

Evie was soon digging in the sand as Sorcha and Quincy sat close by. Quincy frequently had to reach out to keep her from putting sand in her mouth.

"So, how does it feel?" Sorcha asked.

"Terrifying. Exciting. Surreal."

Sorcha laughed. "You look normal. Actually—" She leaned forward to see his face closer. "You look softer. Happier."

"Wow. That's shocking. I feel like a mess."

"Well, that too. But a happy mess."

"Thanks for offering to make dinner. I've just been grabbing sandwiches or eating what she's eating. A home-cooked meal sounds heaven-sent."

"Well, I am heaven-sent," Sorcha teased. He laughed, and the sound warmed her from head to toe, even more than the setting Florida sun.

Once Evie grew tired of the sand, they stood and dusted themselves off.

Quincy picked Evie up and hugged her to his chest. "Ready to go home, Evie?"

She nodded, but Sorcha wasn't sure if the little girl understood his words or just wanted to make her daddy happy.

It didn't matter, either way. But it filled Sorcha's heart to see them together. She reminded herself that she couldn't get emotionally attached to them. She would go home in a couple of weeks, and she needed to figure out what was next with her career. So many things on her plate right now. It was probably a good thing that Quincy had his hands full with his daughter. He couldn't even think about a relationship.

Quincy gave Evie a bath as Sorcha started dinner. He couldn't get over the enjoyment on Evie's face as she splashed in the tub, chasing bubbles. Her smiles eased the doubt in his mind. She seemed to accept his limitations as a father. Maybe he could be the dad she needed.

Once Evie was clean and dressed in her footed pajamas, he let her waddle out to the kitchen.

"I'll heat her dinner up," he said.

"Wouldn't it be better to feed her, then give her a bath?" Sorcha asked.

Huh. He didn't want to admit it, but that made sense. "She doesn't make a mess."

"OK, cowboy."

"Cowboy?"

"It's the wild west in here. Baths, then dinner? Next thing you know, she'll be driving your car at the age of seven."

"There's something wrong with that?" He put Evie in the highchair and gave her a few toddler crackers to munch on, hoping crumbs wouldn't get all over her pajamas. "It smells good in here."

"Thanks. Keep your expectations low. But I hope you'll like it. It's my one specialty."

"What do you do for dinner the other six nights of the week?"

"Ha. Well, Linda cooks a couple of meals, we eat out a couple nights a week, and then there is always cereal."

"Yeah?"

"Or eggs. Pancakes. I love breakfast for dinner."

"What do you eat for breakfast?" He found the homemade nuggets he'd made with four different vegetables for Evie. It was one of the many recipes the foster family had sent along with her. He wished he had their address so he could send them a thank-you.

"Coffee. A banana and a granola bar. On school days, anyway. I'm usually in such a rush in the morning. I am not a morning person."

"Not surprised. I see your late hours here."

"I'm on vacation here."

"True. Are you different at home?"

"Not much." She shrugged. "What are you feeding Evie? Could she have some spaghetti?"

"Well, that *would* probably require a second bath, so let's hold off on the red sauce."

"Oh...right. Good call."

Sorcha stood at the stove, stirring the saucepan. Quincy danced around her as he prepared dinner for Evie.

Sorcha was playing music on her phone, and Evie bopped around in the highchair.

Evie finished eating before their dinner was ready, so Quincy took her out of the highchair and put her down so she could wobble about.

A few minutes later, Sorcha asked for the garlic-butter mixture she'd brought, and Quincy reached into the fridge to grab it. He turned to see Evie standing next to Sorcha with her tiny hand on Sorcha's leg. Sorcha was talking to Evie, and they had their eyes locked on each other.

His heart squeezed at the sight. He hardly knew Sorcha, but she had slid right into his life like a baseball player stealing home. A player on *his* team. When did he become a team player? He'd spent most of his life content with playing solo. The odd one out, a solitaire man in a gin rummy world.

He'd watched his contemporaries partner up; slowly at first, then like an avalanche, everyone was hooked-up and settled-down. At thirty, he still thought he'd find the right one and partner up himself. And he had at thirty-seven, but his marriage to Suze was over quicker than he could have imagined. After that, he'd given up on the idea.

For the first time in a long time, he imagined what it would be like to have a partner again. Someone who could make him laugh when the world seemed against him. Someone who had his back, like Sorcha. She'd clearly been fighting for him all this time, trying to get him on a date, helping him get ready for his daughter's arrival. She could've turned and run when she found out about Evie, but she'd stepped up to the plate. She was a fighter.

He had to get that thought out of his head. First of all, Sorcha didn't live here and would leave. Besides, she deserved to fall in love with someone without complications, someone good enough for her. He wasn't that person.

"Right, Q?"

"What?"

Sorcha twisted to look at him. "I told Evie if she keeps tugging on my shorts, someone's going to get an eye full." Man, I don't need that thought in my head. "Right. Here we go, little lady. Let's let Sorcha cook without you underfoot." He picked Evie up, taking a moment to smell the sauce simmering on the stove as an excuse to stand close to Sorcha. Her freshly washed hair still had the lingering minty scent of her shampoo, mixed with a coconut fragrance.

After dinner, Quincy prepared a bottle of milk for Evie and took her to the rocking chair in the living room. Sitting down with her in his lap, he placed a small pink blanket around her shoulders and rocked her as he gave her the bottle.

Sorcha cleaned the kitchen, putting food away, washing dishes, and even wiping down all the surfaces.

He watched her, glancing between the beautiful woman in the kitchen and the sweet little girl in his lap.

What has happened to my life? This scene of domestic tranquility is right out of a TV sitcom. We just need some audience laughter and a director yelling "Cut!" to finish the scene. Gazing at the front door, he imagined a small TV studio holding an audience.

He wanted to tell Sorcha to stop cleaning, that he'd get it later. He didn't want to take advantage of her, but a part of him enjoyed it. She seemed happy. He could hear her humming softly. He didn't know the name of the song, but he recognized it as a current pop hit that got played on the jukebox in the bar, a frequent pick of the young clientele.

A soft grunt from Evie drew his attention back to his daughter. He shifted her closer, and she reached up, grabbing his beard. She tugged gently and didn't let go. Her eyes drifted shut, and she continued drinking the milk, but she slowed down.

Sorcha must have tiptoed from the kitchen because he didn't hear her approach. She placed a hand on his shoulder. Looking at Evie, she scrunched her face in an "Oh my heavens, how adorable" look. She mouthed the question, "Need anything?"

He shook his head no. He was content, a word he wasn't accustomed to using to describe his state of mind.

He could get used to this feeling, even if he didn't deserve it.

Chapter 15

Sorcha poured herself a glass of water as Quincy carried Evie to the bedroom.

Quincy said his rental lease is up this fall. Good thing, because he really needs a bigger place with a separate bedroom for Evie. At least he doesn't have a lot of stuff to move. He could rent a small van and move all his possessions in one quick trip. Funny how that would be mostly baby things.

She moved to the living-room couch, picking up a white teddy bear. It was crazy to think about how upended Quincy's life had become; in just a couple of weeks, he'd gone from being a bachelor with few cares in the world to a single dad with a tiny human to care for in a blink of an eye.

Sorcha wanted kids but hadn't contemplated having a stepchild. Barb, her stepmom, had done a decent job stepping into the role. She'd been warm and caring to Sorcha but not overreaching, which Sorcha would have hated. Barb knew she'd never take the place of Sorcha's mom, yet she'd tried to fill at least a sliver of the gap, if not the entire hole.

Teaching almost two hundred kids over the course of her career had given Sorcha plenty of experience with eight-year-olds, but this toddler experience was new.

Quincy closed the door to the bedroom and walked with quiet steps into the kitchen. "I think she's down."

"Good."

"Getting a nightcap. Want something?"

"Sure. Whatever you're having."

Quincy poured whiskey into two rocks glasses and came to the couch. He handed her one, holding his glass out to clink.

"Cheers."

"Cheers to putting the little lady down, Daddy-O."

Quincy grinned at her as he sat beside her on the couch, letting out a long sigh before taking a sip of the amber liquid.

"That is the strangest label. Dad."

"Sure. But it has a nice ring to it. I think you're going to grow into it nicely."

Quincy leaned forward to put his glass on the coffee table, then leaned back, closing his eyes and resting his head on the back of the couch. "Peace."

"Does that mean I can't talk?"

"You can talk. Don't expect a lot of response. I'm beat."

"Understandable. She's a busy little thing. Running, exploring, babbling. She's going to be singing before you know it."

Sorcha paused, studying Quincy's face. She wanted to reach out and run her finger down his face, starting at his hairline and following the path between his eyes, over his nose, his mouth, and ending in the coarse hairs of his beard. She imagined taking out a sketch pad and sketching his profile. Not having touched a sketchpad in years, she would be rusty, but it would be fun to attempt again.

"Talk to me or I'll fall asleep," Quincy said, keeping his eyes closed.

"It wouldn't be good to fall asleep in that position. Imagine the neck pain tomorrow. What do you want me to talk about?"

"Anything that doesn't have to do with parenting. Tell me things I don't know about you."

Well, she was an expert on her own life. She could probably talk for hours.

"Wow. Where to start? I'll start with my family. Happy childhood. Great parents. Oops, I said the p-word, sorry about that. Anyway, my mom died when I was twenty. I was in college, and it was devastating. I'm proud of myself for finishing and getting my degree. There were plenty of days when I thought I couldn't."

Sorcha huffed out a breath. "She was the best mom. She always had my back and encouraged me to try new things. We'd take the train to Chicago for mom and daughter dates. We would visit museums, go to lunch, and shop. Pure magic.

"She loved art, so we frequented the art museums. Especially the Art Institute, but we went to all of them. The Ukrainian Institute, the Museum of Contemporary Art, the DePaul Art Museum, and, well, you get the idea. She wanted to be a curator, and she inspired me to follow in her footsteps.

"But when she died, I decided I would pursue education. I would have needed a master's degree to be a curator, and I didn't have the drive left."

Quincy hadn't moved since she'd started talking. She moved forward and touched his arm softly.

"I'm listening."

"Just checking. Anyway, at least I still work with art. Mostly involving finger-paints, coloring books, and popsicle sticks."

Quincy's cheek lifted in a half-smile. "You said you wanted a career change. Could you do that now?"

Sorcha leaned back. She had some financial leeway now, with her inheritance, but was that what she wanted to do?

"Maybe. Going back to school is a big commitment, and I would miss having a steady paycheck."

"Why not both? Work and study?"

"But that would be even more time away from my social life, and you know how important that is to me."

"Yet you're here alone."

"No, I'm not. I'm with you, silly."

"This is no social life." He sat up and reached for his tumbler. "I've roped you into babysitting for me and helping me interview nannies."

He leaned forward, his arms resting on his knees. His head bent forward, and a scowl creased his brow.

Sorcha put her hand on his shoulder. "Hey, I'm having fun. I'm happy to help. Don't feel guilty about it."

Quincy tossed back the remaining liquid in his glass and set down the empty cup.

Sorcha looked at the tumbler in her hand. She took another small sip; the whiskey burned as it slid down her throat.

"Keep talking." He resumed the resting position on the couch.

"Hey." Sorcha scooted backwards on the couch, sitting sideways with her back against the armrest. "Lie back. Head here." She patted the side of her leg. "I'll massage your scalp. It will relax you."

He turned his face towards her and raised an eyebrow.

"I'm serious," she said, answering the question he didn't ask. "I'm good at this. Ask my friends."

Quincy just shook his head, but he complied. Once his head was on her leg, he stretched his legs out, the back of his knees propped on the other armrest.

She began smoothing her thumbs across his forehead, willing the furrowed brow to relax. She pretended she was washing his hair in the sink like a hairdresser would.

"I'll continue my stories. My dad is a good man. He remarried a few years ago, so I have a stepmom and two stepbrothers. They're fine."

She paused a moment, unsure about saying the next part. "My dad just informed me I have a little inheritance money from my mom. He's kept that info from me for ten years, but I guess I'll forgive him."

Quincy chuckled. "That's nice."

"Yes, I paid off my student loans and put some cash in the bank. He suggested I buy a nice little starter home. His words. In their neighborhood. Isn't that silly?"

"Not if that's what you want."

"Well, as a single man, what would you think of a woman with her own house? Would it be a turnoff?"

"Not at all. I'd be impressed."

"Hmm. Interesting. Good to know." She used her fingernails to scratch his head.

He let out a low moan.

Sorcha smiled, though he couldn't see her. "Feels good, doesn't it?"

"Amazing. I'm in danger of falling asleep, though." He sat up and moved next to Sorcha. He rested his head on her shoulder in an unexpected move.

"Again, with the odd neck angle." She shimmied her shoulder softly to tease him, but did not want him to move. The weight of his head was comforting. Grounding.

"Maybe you should be a chiropractor. You seem to be into body alignment."

"Hmm," Sorcha considered. "Maybe. But that would require too much schooling. I hope I'm done with that."

"You're done, and I was just starting."

"Just starting? What do you mean?"

"I took a class through the local community college this spring."

"Yeah?"

"Don't get too excited. Just exploring some ideas. Thought I might get into restaurant management, and some business classes would help. But now..." His voice trailed off, and Sorcha knew he was thinking about taking care of Evie.

"Don't give up! You can do both. Slow and steady gets the worm. Or something like that."

Quincy sat up straight and looked at her. A smile started at the left side of his mouth, slowly making its way across. "You're optimistic. I don't have a lot of that in my life. It's refreshing."

"I can be refreshing," she said, her voice lifting breezily.

Quincy's incredible blue eyes shifted from her eyes to her mouth, and Sorcha's lungs froze. *Breathe, body, breathe. He's going to kiss me! Don't pass out!*

His eyes slid back to hers, asking the question that had an obvious answer, *Yes!*

She didn't move. Didn't blink. She waited.

Quincy leaned forward as he tilted his head. When his lips finally met hers, it felt like she'd won the fifty/fifty raffle at the ballpark for thousands of dollars. She'd bought a ticket with a faint hope that she'd win, but the winning was even better than she could have expected.

She returned the kiss, enjoying the slow pace. Quincy reached up and cupped the side of her face, not to keep her in place, but to deepen the contact. His thumb stroked her cheek slowly. She felt adored.

Far too soon, he applied a little extra pressure to her lips and pulled back, his eye contact steady and anticipatory.

Now it was her turn for a slow smile. She wanted to ask if she was refreshing, but that would be too bold.

"Sorcha," he said, shaking his head. "You are..." He paused, considering his words. "Something." He leaned back and shook his head again. "It's too bad our timing is off."

"What do you mean, off?"

"You're a handful, and I've already got my hands full trying to figure out how I'm going to raise Evie. I can't do both. Besides, you don't live here."

She wanted to make a retort, but he was right.

Quincy stood. "It's late. Evie gets up early."

Sorcha popped up. "Yep. I'll go. What are you doing tomorrow? Need any help?"

"We're taking a ride. Going to meet up with my sister."
"Oh? Where does she live?"
"Orlando. Land of magic."
"Ha. Nice. Enjoy."
"Are you going to call for a rideshare?"
"No. I'll walk on the beach. Look at the stars."
"I'll see you Monday for dinner, right?"
"Yes, of course. Good night."

Stepping outside, she closed her eyes and took a deep breath of the fresh evening air. She remembered the look on Quincy's face as he pulled back from the kiss. Her body tingled with the memory. A smile spread across her face until she remembered his words about bad timing. She opened her eyes and frowned. He was going to be a challenge. Good thing she wasn't afraid of challenges.

The walk back to the Mockingbird was quiet; only a few people were strolling and one man was jogging, which gave Sorcha time to reflect on the evening.

Quincy had opened up to her a bit, but he was still a mystery. Every time she thought she had him pegged, he would say something that made her reassess. Like his comment about taking a college course. She would never have guessed that.

While he didn't seem thrilled with bartending, he didn't seem concerned about his career choice. Sorcha found it interesting that he'd started classes before he knew about his daughter.

She thought he might be even more motivated to study, maybe to get a degree to increase his chances of a higher salary, now that he had a child to care for.

Those thoughts flitted through her mind quickly, cataloging the information to add to her picture of Quincy.

She turned her thoughts to the kiss, replaying it over and over to seal it permanently in her memory bank. Her body still buzzed from the unexpected and mind-blowing kiss. The sand under her feet seemed to propel her forward instead of challenging her movement.

He was the first man with a full beard she'd ever kissed. It might have been ticklish, but she was so focused on the pressure from his lips and the way he touched her face that she'd paid little attention to the beard. She'd missed her chance to run her fingers through it. Maybe next time. If there was a next time.

Chapter 16

"Less than a week in the daddy job and you act like a pro already."

Quincy handed Evie a small doll with a plastic baby bottle, and Evie attempted to feed it.

It was so stinking cute. Sorcha smiled to watch Evie babble as she played with the doll.

The restaurant's dark interior was cozy and cool. On a Monday evening there were few customers which suited their party well. Sorcha was a little nervous about how Evie would behave in a restaurant and hoped they wouldn't get too many disapproving stares.

It turned out her fears were unfounded. Evie was well-behaved, and Quincy was a champ at anticipating his baby's needs and heading off any potential meltdowns.

"I'm thankful I've had four straight days with her. Lucky the bar could switch my shifts around."

Sorcha reached for a roll in the breadbasket. "Are you ready to start the babysitter interviews?"

"I'm ready to have help. I can't afford not to work, though by the time I pay for a sitter, I might be lucky to break even. But I'll figure it out."

"Being a single parent is challenging. Can you get financial support?"

"Only as a last resort. I can and will earn my way."

"Don't doubt it. Well, I'm here to help with babysitting until you can hire someone."

"Thank you, again."

The server approached with their salads and drinks. "You two have the cutest baby." She put their items on the table. When she placed Sorcha's salad too close to the highchair, Evie launched forward with the doll tightly clutched in her reaching hand. The doll ended up in the middle of the salad plate.

"Oops!" Sorcha said, laughing. "Baby fall down." She lifted the doll, its face covered in ranch dressing.

Grabbing her napkin, she wiped the doll's face.

"I'm so sorry!" The server offered to bring a fresh salad and hurried away with the doll-mushed plate.

"Whoa," Quincy said, shaking a finger in front of Evie. "Food is for eating, not playing."

The little girl leaned back in her seat, her eyes wide. "No?" she said, shaking her head.

"No."

Sorcha worried the tot would start crying. "It's OK! All better." She handed the doll back to Evie. "That was unexpected," she said to Quincy.

"She's quick. You got to be quicker."

"I take it you're getting some practice."

"Plenty. It's like I'm dodging a minefield every waking minute."

"But you seem to enjoy it. I think you're actually more relaxed than you were before she arrived."

"You think?"

"Yes. At the risk of offending your masculinity and as I said before, I think you're softer."

"I would never admit to being soft," Quincy said, leaning forward, with a crooked smile. "But yeah, with Evie I feel...different."

Sorcha agreed. A part of him was softer, quieter. More relaxed. Gentler. Taking care of his daughter was smoothing out his rougher edges.

And it looked good on him.

Quincy huffed. "But don't tell anyone. I don't know if I am softer. I feel more alert than ever. It's like all my senses have gone into overdrive. I'm always assessing threats and risks. And if someone looks twice at her, my shoulders pinch and I'm ready to go to battle if needed."

"Oh, that's adorable. Papa Bear in fight mode." She knew he'd be an intense, raving grizzly bear if someone threatened Evie's safety.

"The rage is real."

Sorcha smiled. "I can imagine."

"Do you want to have kids?"

Whoa. His change of direction made her head spin.

"Absolutely." She sighed. "My roommate, Linda, and I have talked about trying to have kids at the same time. You know, be mom friends raising kid friends, but I don't think she's going to wait around for me to find someone, fall in love, get engaged, get married, then start. She'll probably be pregnant by Christmas."

Quincy's brow furrowed, and his lip twitched down. "She's the one getting married down here?"

"Yes, on the beach in front of the Mockingbird; the building is special to both of them. The wedding is July sixth." She bit her lip and looked down. Should she ask? "Want to go with me?"

His eyes widened. Sorcha had expected surprise, and he didn't disappoint.

"Yeah?" His eyes went to Evie.

"She could come, too!" Sorcha hadn't asked Linda, but Evie was a baby. Where else was she going to be?

"What a great wedding guest. A single man with his child."

"It would be great. Everyone loves babies."

"I'm not sure brides feel that way. All eyes should be on the bride on her wedding day."

"Well, there is that." Sorcha nodded.

He was going to say no. A pit opened in her stomach. He'd just told her on Saturday night that their timing was all wrong. Sure, there were hurdles, but she thought they could have something.

It was probably for the best, but she couldn't help but feel disappointed he wouldn't be there.

She'd never had an easy time figuring out what men were thinking, where they thought the relationship was going. She'd been surprised so many times when one hadn't called her back when they'd said they would or when they only called in the middle of the night.

If a guy goes to a wedding with you, it must mean something. Right? If he came, it would mean he wanted to spend time with Sorcha. It would be one of the first times he'd be with her because he wanted to be. Up to now, she'd either forced the time with him by sitting in the bar while he was working or by talking him into seeing her outside of Crabbie's.

Their dinners arrived, and she took turns with Quincy to eat and to entertain Evie. Quincy had fed Evie her meal before they left the house, so she didn't need to eat at the restaurant.

Oh well, she hadn't planned on a date for the wedding. Nothing had changed.

Who am I kidding? Everything had changed.

Quincy, whom she'd found intriguing and handsome, was sneaking into her psyche, slipping past her defenses like Cupid's arrow, aiming for her heart.

And now Evie! How would her heart survive the onslaught of all that sweetness and cuteness?

She'd been happy to extend her stay to help Quincy, but at what risk to herself?

If she wasn't careful, she was going to leave Seaside Bay with a sunburn, an ache for a little girl she'd just met, and a giant crater in her soul which would remain when Quincy was out of her life.

She forked the last bite of pasta on her plate and realized Quincy hadn't corrected the server about *their* baby. She glanced at the adorable child, and her heart melted. Evie was a precocious child, full of laughter and joy. Sorcha hoped that someday she'd be lucky enough to have a little girl just like Evie.

Quincy pulled up to the curb outside the Mockingbird, and Sorcha reached down to pick up her handbag from the floor.

"Thanks for dinner. I had a lot of fun with you two." She looked into the back seat. "Good night, Evie, sweetie. I'll see you tomorrow."

"Thanks for going with us. Our first meal out of the house, and I think it was a success."

"For reals. What time do you want me tomorrow?"

Her words stirred an eagerness inside Quincy. He knew she meant for the interviews, but that was not the first thought that had jumped into his head.

"Ten. First interview at ten-thirty."

"Good. We can put our game plan together then. You know, who's going to ask what? What are the critical questions to ask?"

"Are you putting together a lesson plan in your head?"

"Maybe?"

He laughed and shook his head. Evie let out an odd moan that he was learning meant she was getting fussy and might cry soon. He'd better get her home.

"That's my cue," he said, nodding towards the back seat.

"Right. Get home safe. Bye again." She kissed her hand and blew the kiss to Evie.

He wished that it was a real kiss for him, but Sorcha hopped out of the car and shut the door. She stood on the sidewalk and waved goodbye.

The light from a streetlamp half a block away lit the lower half of her body. She wore a short, flouncy skirt that fluttered in the gulf breeze. The heels she wore forced her calves into a flex that defined them nicely. Her face was in shadow, but he'd spent the last hour memorizing the fullness of her lips, the shape of her eyes, the fleck of gold in her irises, and the pertness of her nose.

He wasn't the type of person to take a lot of photos. His memory served him well enough. In the last few days he'd probably taken a hundred photos of Evie, sending several to his mom and sister, who'd sent back countless emojis and demanded more.

Now he realized he needed a photo of Sorcha.

In a few short weeks, memories would be all he had left of her. She'd return home, and he knew as well as his middle name was Peter that she would find a normal guy to fall in love with. She'd probably return to Seaside Bay in the spring with her fiancé on her arm.

Not that it mattered. He'd be long gone by spring. On to the next map-pin location. Hopefully, she'd be out of his mind at that point, but he had doubts.

Once he saw Sorcha enter the lobby of the condo building, he turned to check on Evie. "Ready to get home, Evie-girl?"

She smiled and cooed at him.

"I'll take that as a yes."

He smiled to himself, realizing he'd spoken more in the last four days than he had in the four weeks prior. He gave Evie the play-by-play for everything he was doing, what they were going to be doing, and what they might do some day in the future.

Maybe someone had told him, maybe it was instinct, but he knew Evie needed to hear him speak in order to learn the language. That was part of it, but the other part was the enjoyment of having someone around. His days were brighter now that Evie had arrived.

The parent role may have come to him unexpectedly, and prior to this week he would have said it wasn't wanted, but once the shock wore off, he found it wasn't so bad after all.

The shock of Evie's existence, and the shock of his feelings for Sorcha, had come so close together that he wondered whether in a few months, he would have trouble remembering who'd come into his life first.

His only regret was that while Evie was stuck with him for the next sixteen years, Sorcha was not.

It would not be easy when Evie grew and flew the coop, but he would have years to prepare for it.

With Sorcha, he wouldn't even get weeks.

Every time he was with her, he found something else to appreciate. He found they had more in common than he'd originally assumed. They'd both lost a parent at a vulnerable time in their lives, they were both thinking about career changes, and they'd both experienced dating nightmares.

She was unlike anyone he'd dated before. He'd originally thought she was out of his league. Now he realized that she'd been right—that was just a story he'd been telling himself. He shouldn't stereotype people by class or background or education. He should just get to know the person and then figure out if they had a kind soul and values that aligned with his. That's all that was important.

Getting to know Sorcha, he realized that she was aligned in all the right ways.

He was going to remind himself of that every day she was here. If their days together were numbered, he was going to make the very best of every one of them.

At dinner, Sorcha had said he was softer. She meant regarding Evie, and he'd answered thinking about Evie, but now he realized Sorcha had somehow bypassed the fortress he'd built around himself. She brought a light and a freshness with her, one he hadn't known he craved.

Maybe he wasn't the most passionate man, but he wasn't dead either.

Chapter 17

After the sixth nanny interview, Quincy shut the door and groaned.

Sorcha didn't want to hear what was wrong with the last interviewee, Kylie. Quincy had said something negative about all of the candidates. Chelsea was too immature, Monica seemed like an airhead, Joan didn't laugh at Sorcha's jokes, Sue said she wouldn't wash dishes, and Ramona had a heavy accent.

Instead of engaging Quincy, she picked Evie up from the floor and walked with her to look at the pictures and items around the room. The toddler loved it when Sorcha pointed and said the words for things: picture, window, chair, curtain, TV, etc. Evie would giggle and point, nodding her head when Sorcha spoke the word.

The morning and interviews had started well. It had been sunny and bright; the air smelled like warm sand and sea water. The first potential nanny arrived in a bright pink blouse with white slacks, which caused Sorcha to question the candidate's understanding of little kids, but she understood the woman was trying to make an impression.

But as the day wore on and they ground through the interviews, the clouds rolled in and a storm threatened.

The grayer the sky got, the grumpier Quincy became.

Quincy walked to the fridge and grabbed a beer. He didn't say so, but Sorcha could tell his frustration was getting to him. Maybe the alcohol would ease some of his tension. She could hope.

After circling the room with Evie, Sorcha asked Quincy if he was getting hungry. He'd said he had burgers to grill, and she'd brought over several vegetables to make a salad.

"I'll start on dinner soon," he said. "I need a few minutes to decompress."

"I understand." Evie wiggled in Sorcha's arms, so she sat her down in front of the bright red barn with assorted animals. "I'll start washing and cutting up vegetables for salad."

Quincy stood with his back against the wall, half in the kitchen and half in the living room, watching Evie.

"I don't know what to do about a sitter," he said, taking a pull from the bottle. "I didn't like any of them."

The black jeans and black T-shirt he wore complemented his dark mood. Sorcha wondered if he was comfortable in the heavy work boots that he liked to wear. She kicked her shoes off the minute she walked in the door.

"I think you're too picky." She ran water in the sink to wash the lettuce, turning slightly to watch him. "Several of them had stellar resumés and seemed like good fits."

"Which?"

"I thought Ramona was fantastic. And Evie went right to her, sat in her lap the whole time. She's worked for several families and had recommendations from all of them."

"Her Spanish accent was pretty thick, though."

"You live in Florida. It would be great for Evie to be bilingual."

"We won't always live here."

"Doesn't matter. There are Spanish-speaking people all over. You said Texas might be next. You don't think there's a large Spanish-speaking population there?" She slammed the head of lettuce down hard on its stem to bust it loose.

"You're right about that."

"We don't in my school, but I know a lot of schools teach Spanish in their grade schools. It's a valuable skill."

"Wow. Didn't know." He rolled his neck, releasing the tension.

"Now you know. And you still need a nanny. Do you want to see more resumés?"

"No."

"All right. Are you ready to decide?"

"No."

Thankful her back was to him and Evie, she rolled her eyes. This was like talking to a third grader who didn't get enough sleep or food.

"Do you think you can hire one of the women we met today?"

"Maybe."

Quincy walked to the garbage can and pitched his bottle. She wasn't surprised when he went to the fridge for a second one.

"Want something?" he asked, standing with the door open.

"Not now. Maybe with dinner."

She was going to try a new tactic. Be quiet. Let him talk when he was ready. This was his problem to solve, and she guessed he wasn't ready for encouragement and cheerfulness right now.

Quincy walked into the living room. As Sorcha turned to grab the carrots to chop, she stole a glance at him. He sat down on the floor and picked up a little sheep. "Baa," he said to Evie, who smiled at him.

At least the baby was oblivious to her daddy's foul mood.

Once the salad was assembled, Sorcha covered the bowl with a clean dish towel and put it in the fridge. She grabbed a bottled iced tea, strolled to the living room, and sat in the recliner. As she rocked, Quincy rolled onto his back, and Evie climbed on his chest. She sat on his pectoral muscles and bounced.

Quincy laughed, and Sorcha let out a sigh. His mood was lifting.

He glanced at Sorcha and gave her a half-smile. "I'm being a grouch, aren't I?"

"A bit."

"Sorry. I don't want to take my frustrations out on you. I just need to get this right."

"Choose one. If it doesn't work out, you can find someone else. Just pick one that you think will do a good job."

"Can't you stay for the summer?" he asked.

She really needed to figure out her job situation. If she returned to teaching in the fall, she probably could stay for the summer. Especially now that she had a little financial nest egg. But if she was to get serious about doing something else, she needed to figure out where she was going to live and be there to interview.

Ugh. My life is in flux. I'm in need of a new job and a new apartment. A new boyfriend would be nice, too, while we're asking.

Evie leaned forward and pulled on Quincy's beard. He let out a soft growl, and she giggled.

That gets me right in the ovaries. Could she be any cuter?

Skirting his question, she said, "I hope that doesn't hurt you, because you are training her to do that, you know."

"Doesn't hurt a bit."

Evie leaned to her left and nearly toppled over. Quincy grasped her waist, lifted her and set her on the floor, handing her a toy horse.

He sat up and locked eyes with Sorcha, his eyes searching, questioning.

She wanted to squirm under his gaze, but she forced herself to sit still.

"Well, I'll get the grill going. Will you keep an eye on Evie?" He stood.

"Of course."

Sorcha slid off the chair to sit on the floor with Evie, who crawled over with a horse in her hand and a sheep in her mouth. "Give me that sheep, Evie, sweetie."

Quincy rustled around in the kitchen, preparing the burgers. Sorcha found his quietness discomforting, but pushed her unease at his poor attitude aside. Evie deserved her attention now. Sorcha sang her a song about being polite and having good manners that she often sang in her classroom. The song was for Evie, but she hoped the message would get through to Quincy.

Her mind wandered to the complication that this arrangement was causing. She needed to keep looking for a new job. Would she have time to do that while she was babysitting Evie for the next week and a half? Quincy wanted to work extra shifts while she could babysit. He'd offered to pay Sorcha, but she'd refused. This is what friends did for each other—helped each other out.

Maybe Quincy would eventually see her as more than a friend. She couldn't get the kiss from Saturday night out of her mind. Yes, the timing was bad for Quincy, but she couldn't help wanting more.

It meant a lot to her when he asked her for help. She knew she'd been persistent in pursuing him, which didn't make her the best babysitting candidate. But he saw past that. As much as he pushed her away, he saw something that he liked and trusted. He saw past her appearance to who she was on the inside. Most guys didn't do that.

She sighed. At least babysitting Evie meant she wouldn't be bored or alone for her longer stay in Florida. She just wished Evie could carry on a conversation. Ah, well. *She will eventually. Hope I'll be able to see it. There are always video calls.*

He exited the house with a plate of burgers and an old busted tumbler filled with dog food, which he dropped into the bowl on the other side of the grill. He knew the stray dog would smell the meat cooking and make his way over, following his nose.

The grill sat behind the house on a small concrete patio. The house was low enough that he could see in through the kitchen window and watch Sorcha interact with his daughter.

Firing up the grill, he realized he must have said something to irritate Sorcha. She'd gone quiet in the living room. He thought back to the interviews, thankful Sorcha had agreed to conduct them with him.

He loved her interactions with the women and her insightful questions about their philosophies on playtime and learning, their diligence around potty training, and half a dozen other things that Quincy hadn't thought to ask.

Her chattiness and outgoing attitude served her well. She put each of the candidates at ease within a few moments. They answered questions with eyes trained closely on Sorcha, only darting over to him when he spoke.

None of the women had asked about the parenting situation. They just assumed Sorcha was the mother and he was the dad. That's why they directed their attention to the beautiful woman by his side.

The fact that Sorcha and Evie were both very blonde, while he had dark hair, likely contributed to their assumption.

Quincy didn't feel the need to clarify the situation. It was awkward, but he would be the person the nanny would talk to once Sorcha returned home.

He found it interesting that he didn't bother to correct the assumption, not when the server made the comment at dinner the night before and not during the nanny interviews today.

He couldn't shake the feeling that he would be judged deficient for being a single dad and found it strange that he cared. He couldn't help that Evie's mother had died, but he felt enormous guilt about it, anyway. It was nice to fantasize about Sorcha being his partner in raising Evie.

He'd hoped she'd consider staying longer than planned, ideally the whole summer, but she hadn't replied after he mentioned it.

Like everyone else in his life, she would stay just long enough to make him want more, and then she'd be gone.

He'd taught himself to be the one to run first. It hurt less that way.

It wouldn't be easy moving with a baby, but he'd figure it out. He'd have more requirements for the next place: a home with two bedrooms, a pleasant neighborhood with young parents, a town with lots of babysitters.

He flipped the burgers and closed the grill lid. He'd brought another beer outside with him, and he took a long pull. *Nothing better than a beer while grilling.*

This was his third drink. It had to be his last for the evening.

After dinner, he'd take Sorcha home. The car ride might help Evie fall asleep for the night. Bonus.

The little thing seemed pretty happy during the day, but nighttime was hard. She'd cry for her mama, and Quincy would have to rock her and talk to her to soothe her.

He wished he could sing to her like Sorcha had done earlier. Maybe he'd get a sound machine or find a lullaby channel on his music service.

Movement in the window caught his eye. He glanced over to see Sorcha standing in front of the sink with Evie in her arms. Sorcha pointed at him, and he could tell she was saying "Dada" to Evie. Evie pointed and waved. He smiled and waved back.

Sorcha had fallen into place so easily. He knew she was more experienced with seven and eight-year-olds, but she'd done great with the toddler. Evie never seemed nervous or upset with Sorcha around.

He wouldn't hope that things could work out with Sorcha. She lived hundreds of miles away, and she hadn't signed up to become a mom before she was even married. Who would?

She was going to fall in love with a fine, upstanding man who would ask her dad for his daughter's hand in marriage after purchasing a five-carat ring for his bride-to-be.

He'd be wealthy, probably a doctor, with a normal name like John. A plastic surgeon. She could be one of those stay-at-home parents who never had to work a day after the wedding. He'd give her a black credit card so she could shop five days a week.

She'd probably cut her shopping back to three days after having the first of their two-point-five kids.

That's what she deserved.

Not a broke biker like himself, a loser who knew the inside of a bar better than most.

She'd only be around for another couple of weeks. He needed to find a nanny. Maybe a follow-up interview or two would set his mind at ease and allow him to make this critical decision.

Evie was precious, and she deserved to be treated like a princess, just not a spoiled one.

The girls walked away from the window, and Quincy checked on the burgers.

Just about done.

Just like his time with Sorcha.

If he only had two more weeks with her, he was going to make the most of it and appreciate her. And not just as a babysitter. He was going to attempt to make their remaining time together memorable.

If he wasn't lucky enough to win Sorcha over, at least he would make darn sure John, or Matt, or Tom had to work extra hard in that department.

He would do whatever he could to make sure Sorcha realized her worth and wouldn't settle for someone who didn't treat her like a queen.

There was no time or budget for big gestures, but he could manage baked goods. There was an amazing bakery north of town. On Friday, he'd take Evie for a drive and buy a nice assortment of goodies for Sorcha's next day of babysitting. That would be the first treat. He'd think of others.

Chapter 18

"I'm telling you; I think it's a great opportunity!" Linda's enthusiasm was contagious. She'd called to tell Sorcha that her sister, Laurel, the principal of a large elementary school in Peoria, was hiring a curriculum specialist. Linda thought Sorcha had the experience Laurel was looking for.

"Wow," Sorcha replied. "It's something to consider."

She'd thought about moving to Peoria if the right job opportunity came along. It would be a pleasant change, and only thirty minutes away from her dad and from Linda.

"At least apply. You can find out more about the position during the interview process." Linda paused. "The only downside is that you'd be working for my sister."

"There is that. How did this come up? Does Laurel know I'm looking?"

"Yes, I told her. Since you're both in elementary education, I thought she might have some leads. I didn't expect it to be in her school. She sent me the link to the job posting. I'll text it to you."

"That sounds great. I'll check it out. What's new with you?"

Linda sighed. "I started packing."

"Ouch. That's hard to hear."

"I know. I didn't want to upset you, but I'm trying to get all the non-essentials packed up. Mason's going to come and help me move what I can this weekend. Can't believe we're getting married in two weeks!" Linda squealed.

Sorcha laughed. "It's going to be a beautiful wedding, celebrating two of the greatest people I know."

"Awe, Sor'. That's sweet. How are things going there?"

"Good. Today's my last day alone, thank goodness. I'm babysitting Evie for the next seven days. We're going to become besties."

"My crown is going to a toddler."

"Hey, you'll still be Bestie Number One."

"And don't you forget it."

"Never."

"Ready?"

"Sure." Sorcha glanced at the childcare books she'd bought. "I've done some research. I have ideas for activities and exercises to do with her. We'll explore. Take walks on the beach. Read. All sorts of fun things."

"Will you be able to keep job-hunting?"

"I'm not watching her twenty-four seven, so yes. I have a plan, and I think that if needed, I'll be able to schedule interviews around my schedule."

"Great. Hope something comes up soon."

"Same." Sorcha looked at the time on her laptop. "I need to run. The day's getting away from me."

They hung up, and Sorcha looked at the notepad next to her. The job Linda had mentioned was interesting. It would use many of her skills, keep her close to education but give her a different focus and increase her skill set. It was appealing.

But it was home. In Illinois.

Far away from Quincy and Evie.

That part was painful. As much as she told herself not to get too attached to either of them, she was finding it harder and harder to imagine a life without seeing them daily.

Her phone beeped. It was a text message from Linda with the link to her sister's job posting.

Sorcha found the job listing and looked it over. It was tempting. She applied online and added that job to the list of jobs she'd applied to.

She'd been on the job hunt all morning. She'd found and applied for sixteen jobs, in a variety of areas; a medical receptionist in a small office, data entry analyst, a research assistant at a university, a community-center youth director, an admissions advisor, and a marketing specialist. The last one was a bit of a stretch and might require some training, but it was an entry-level position with a local retail boutique, and she would appreciate the employee discount. Most of the positions were in Illinois. That seemed the most logical.

But two of them were in Florida. One was teaching fourth grade in Clearwater, the other was teaching third grade in Tampa. There were no openings here in Seaside Bay, but that didn't surprise her because it was a small elementary school.

Not that she had a compelling reason to move here. Quincy seemed pretty adamant that he was moving, but she liked to consider the option.

Sorcha didn't even try to stay awake until Quincy got home on Friday night. He was closing the bar, and the 2:00 a.m. closing time was way past her bedtime, now that she was busy watching Evie.

She'd found an extra blanket in the linen closet and grabbed a pillow off Quincy's bed. She held the pillow to her face and smiled at the soap scent of fresh air and fir trees. Quincy's scent. The couch wasn't the most comfortable temporary bed, but it would have to do. She'd considered crawling into his bed, but it felt too forward; she didn't want to presume he'd care for the company.

She figured if she was asleep on the couch, he could wake her or not wake her when he got home. It wouldn't matter; she was nervous about walking back to the condo building this late at night, but she had pepper spray on her key chain and knew how to use it if necessary.

When Quincy walked in the front door, her eyes sprang open and she sat up quickly.

She'd left the light above the kitchen sink on when she laid down, so there was plenty of light to see that it was Quincy and not an intruder.

"Hi," she said, rubbing her eyes.

"Sorry to wake you." He hung his keys on a hook by the door.

"Not a problem." She yawned and sat up. "I'm a light sleeper."

"Good to know. I think."

Sorcha laughed. "How was work?"

"Busy. Good tips."

Quincy walked past her and got a glass of water out of the kitchen before coming back and sitting beside her on the couch.

He smelled like beer and whiskey, a long night in the bar.

He took a drink of water and set the glass on the end table. "How was Evie? Any trouble getting her to sleep?"

"She was great, no trouble at all. I rocked her in the chair for a little while and she dozed off. Didn't wake up when I put her in the crib."

"Glad to hear."

"I left you a note on the kitchen table with, um—" She yawned again. "Our activities and what she ate today." She shook her head. "I should get going."

"It's late. Why don't you stay?"

"And sleep on this couch? No, thanks."

"I didn't mean to sleep here." He looked towards the bedroom door. "With me."

"Um. As tempting as that sounds, I don't think it's a good idea. It might confuse Evie."

She'd thought about this. She'd come up with several reasons why staying in his bed was not a good idea. Evie was the first on the list but not the only heart she was looking to protect.

"Yeah. You're right." Quincy sighed and leaned his head back. "Why don't we just sit here and fall asleep like this?"

"You are determined to ruin your neck, aren't you?"

Sorcha pushed the blanket off her lap and began to stand, but Quincy reached out and grasped her hand. "Stay. For a couple minutes. Please?"

"Well, since you said please."

"Here."

Quincy patted the space next to him on the couch, and she scooted closer to him. He put his arm around her and pulled her to his side, placing a kiss on her temple.

"Did I thank you sufficiently for sacrificing your vacation time to help me out with Evie?"

She started to say yes, of course, but teased him instead. "Well, I think you did. You left me cupcakes today."

"And I told you I drove to Venice Gardens to get them."

"Such sacrifice."

"Only the best for my friends."

Aw. "I'm looking forward to tomorrow's surprise."

"Making me up my game, are you now?"

"Of course. Now, I need to go so I can wash my face, put my pajamas on, and crawl into bed."

Quincy pulled her into a full hug and rested his head on her shoulder. "Stop. You're putting visions in my head that don't belong there," he mumbled into her shoulder. She had no trouble understanding what he said.

She wrapped her arms around him and squeezed, but didn't address his comment. He was tired; she was tired. "Your daughter will probably be up early. You should get to bed."

Quincy pulled back from her but didn't let her go. "You're pretty amazing."

"You could have stopped at pretty."

Quincy smiled and shook his head. He closed his eyes and leaned forward to kiss her.

Knowing this was probably a mistake, she still returned his kiss. He tasted like coffee, his means of staying awake so late in the evening. She hoped he'd be able to fall asleep soon and get some rest before Evie woke up.

Sorcha reached up and touched his beard. His skin underneath was warm. She rubbed her palm across his beard and into his hair.

Too soon, Quincy pulled back and quickly kissed her nose. "You are not pretty."

She pulled back, searching to see if he was teasing. "What?"

"You're beautiful."

"Aw. Thank you. Now I can go back to the condo and sleep easy."

"You'll text me when you get back?"

"Yes. But I hope you're asleep before I get there."

"Not likely."

Sorcha stood up, grabbed her tote bag, and pulled her keys out of the side pocket, getting the defense spray in hand. She walked to the door and slipped on her shoes. "Night, Poppa Q."

Quincy had stretched out on the couch. "Safe home, Sorcha."

He was probably asleep before the door closed. Sorcha's walk back to the Mockingbird was uneventful. She marveled at the number of stars in the sky and relished the cooling breeze from the Gulf.

She texted Quincy after she washed her face. He didn't respond, which was fine with her. She was glad he was tired enough to fall asleep quickly.

She wasn't as lucky. Thoughts of Quincy's lips and his kiss kept racing through her mind as sleep evaded her.

Chapter 19

Quincy kicked off the sports slides that he'd reluctantly bought at Sorcha's urging when they'd gone shopping for baby things. When he'd confessed that he only owned the one pair of boots, she'd laughed and said a man living as close as he did to the beach needed sandals. He only gave in to her demand when he saw the basic slide, without painful toe posts.

Sorcha had packed a picnic lunch, and they were on the beach with an extra-large blanket, the food, and a beach canopy Sorcha had borrowed from the Mockingbird building manager.

Once he slathered Evie in sunscreen, he sat her down on the edge of the blanket with a bucket of sand toys, still in the beach umbrella's shade and within arm's reach.

"Do you want tuna salad or ham and cheese?" Sorcha held up one of each sandwich for him to choose.

"Whichever one you don't want."

She tilted her head to one side, considering. Her shoulder-length hair brushed against her bare shoulders. She wore a strapless blue bikini, which had made Quincy's eyes bulge out of his head when she'd pulled off her loose cover-up.

He'd quickly turned his attention to Evie and refused to watch Sorcha apply her own sunscreen. Of course, he was happy to apply lotion to her back. The warmth of her skin was comforting, and he didn't want to stop, but once he'd put on two coats, he thought she'd yell at him if he tried a third.

Shaking the memory from his head, he reached out and took the sandwich she offered. She didn't say which one he was getting, but it didn't matter.

He'd fed Evie before they left the house, but that didn't keep the little girl from coming over to see what he was eating. She plopped down on his lap and asked for a bite. She nibbled the corner of his sandwich and stood up, smacking her lips. "Um," she said, returning to her toys.

He took his own bite, discovered it was tuna, and agreed with his daughter's assessment. "Thanks again for putting lunch together," he said before taking another bite.

"My pleasure. I'm glad you agreed to get together today."

"Sunday Funday."

"Sunday Funday, then you got to work, day." Sorcha sang the words, slightly off-key, but very sweet.

"True."

"Ready for six more days of work before your weekend off?"

"Knowing Evie is with you, I can say yes. Now, next week, when the nanny starts, I'll be a knot of nerves."

"Did you decide yet?"

He'd asked two of the women to come back for a second interview without Sorcha, and he'd decided on Friday. "Yes. Ramona."

"Awesome. I think she'll be great."

"Same. I should have trusted your recommendation on the first day."

"You live, you learn." Sorcha shrugged, giving him an enormous smile. "When will she start?"

"Next Monday."

"Great. You'll have to let me know how it goes. Not that I can rush back and rescue you if it doesn't work out."

"I know. Don't remind me."

Quincy didn't like to think about the fact that Sorcha was going home on Saturday. Yes, she'd come back next week, but that was only for four days, and she'd be busy with her best friend's wedding. He'd be lucky if he got to see her outside of the wedding.

Sorcha had breached his armor, like he'd feared she would. He'd tried to resist her, but it was too late. He was smitten.

Sighing, he looked out at the Gulf. The water churned a darker blue than usual. He looked towards the sky to see if there was a storm in the distance. Nothing. Good. He didn't like the idea of a storm when Sorcha and Evie were alone in the house.

More things to worry about.

He watched as she tossed a small ball towards Evie. Evie didn't catch it, but she grabbed it when it landed and brought it back to Sorcha.

He still didn't believe he deserved Sorcha, and he wouldn't dare hope that things would work out between them.

So, he was going to do what he always did. Focus on the here and now. No sense in dreaming about a future he couldn't control.

When they got back to Quincy's place, Quincy hurried to the bathroom to take a shower to wash off the sand and to get ready for work.

Sorcha put away the leftovers and sat Evie on the side of the sink so she could rinse the sand off the little one's legs and arms. She'd give her a proper bath closer to bedtime, but this was good enough for now.

While she was drying Evie off, Quincy came out of the bedroom with wet hair and fresh clothes.

"I brought a change of clothes for Evie," he said, handing Sorcha a clean pair of pink shorts and a matching pink T-shirt.

"Good." Sorcha tossed the towel she'd used on Evie onto the counter. "I rinsed her off in the sink. I'll take her out the back door and shake out the sand from her clothes before putting her in these."

"In the sink? Clever."

Quincy opened a lower cabinet and grabbed a plastic container. Sorcha couldn't see what was inside of it.

She picked Evie up. "Come on, Miss Sandy. Time to get you in clean clothes."

Evie nodded, and Sorcha went out the back door.

It wasn't a large backyard, but it seemed big enough to Sorcha. They were so close to the beach, why bother keeping up a yard to play in?

Sorcha sat on the single step and put Evie in her lap. "Arms up. Top off."

Evie complied, and Sorcha got her sandy clothes off. As she was putting the clean clothes on Evie, Quincy opened the door behind her.

"Do you have enough room?" Sorcha asked, seeing he wanted to come outside. She leaned away from the door, ensuring she had a good hold on Evie.

"Yep."

Quincy stepped outside with two large cups in his hand. He walked towards the grill and leaned over, dumping food into two dishes that she hadn't noticed before.

"What are you doing?" she asked.

"There are a couple of strays that hang around. A dog and two orange cats. I feed them." He looked sheepish.

"They hang around because you feed them." She teased.

"Maybe. I don't mind. You haven't noticed them?"

"Maybe. A short, ugly yellowish dog?"

"That's Max."

She smiled. "Uh oh. You named it? It's your dog now, buddy."

"Not mine. A stray."

Sorcha laughed. "You name it, you bought it. Did you name the cats, too?"

Quincy looked uncomfortable; Sorcha found it endearing.

"Never mind," she said. "I can tell you did. You own them, too."

Quincy glanced at his phone. "Well, look at that. I got to go to work."

"Ha. Way to dodge the conversation." She pulled the clean T-shirt over Evie's head.

Quincy bent over and placed a kiss on Evie's head. "Bye, Evie. Be good for Sorcha."

Sorcha turned her head towards Quincy to say bye. He kissed her cheek. "Later, Sorcha."

"Bye." She wanted to put her hand to her cheek. *That was unexpected.*

Movement caught her attention, and she turned towards the grill. A large orange cat crept towards the food bowl.

"Hmm," Sorcha whispered, leaning close to Evie's ear. "Look, Eves. Kitty cat."

Evie pointed. "Kiki."

"Yep. Kiki. I wonder what his name is. Your daddy didn't share that info."

The cat seemed to notice them then and slunk off. "Sorry, kitty. We'll go in and let you eat."

Inside, Sorcha put Evie on the living room floor beside the red barn and farm animals. "Sit here one sec and I'll toss these clothes in your hamper."

Evie picked up a sheep and said, "Kiki."

"No, not kiki." Sorcha laughed. "Sheep. Baa."

"Baa. Beep."

"Close enough." Sorcha glanced at the clock. Evie's bedtime was in three hours. She hoped with the sun, sand, and fresh air, she might get her to sleep in two, though that might mean an early morning for Quincy.

For the next couple hours, she and Evie entertained themselves with books, toys, a late dinner, a bubble bath, and a bottle of milk.

When she got Evie to sleep after only fifteen minutes in the rocking chair (that fresh air was a bedtime blessing!), she straightened up the living room. Quincy didn't need to come home to a floor full of small toys and scattered books. She made a cup of herbal tea, grabbed her laptop, and sat on the floor to check email. She didn't expect any response to her applications over the weekend, but it didn't hurt to look.

She glanced around. The house was clean, quiet, and comfortable.

She knew she wanted "this", this cozy home life, with a little one, *someday*. But something was calling her to this *now*. Was it her biological clock telling her it was time, now that she'd turned thirty?

Or was it a handsome bartender with a brooding look and dark tattoos?

Then again, maybe it was the super-sweet little girl with the bright smile and eager expression?

How was she going to go home and leave this?

Pushing that thought aside, she opened her email service. She had five more days to spend here with Evie. She'd enjoy it while she could.

Chapter 20

Evie leaned forward and splashed the water in the pool. She was sitting in a donut-shaped baby float with an awning cover to shield her from the sun. Even with the protection, Sorcha had slathered the child with sunscreen from the top of her head to the tips of her toes. Sorcha stood in the pool, holding onto the float, keeping a close watch on the toddler.

Rosalie was floating in the pool in her own donut float, a much larger one, while Winnie sat in a chair three inches from the edge of the pool, chatting to them all.

"Want another water?" Winnie asked.

"I'm good." Rosalie adjusted herself on the float and pushed off from the edge.

Sorcha spun slightly, so Evie could see Rosalie, her newfound pool buddy. She giggled every time Rosalie pretended to accidentally fall off her float, landing face-first in the water. Rosalie would make a big production of it, flailing her arms and hooting in an exaggerated call.

"So, Quincy must be sad that you're heading home and hanging up your babysitter hat," Winnie said, splashing the water with her feet.

Sorcha thought about Quincy's handsome face when he'd left for work. She could tell it was hard for him to leave Evie, but he had said he was thankful Sorcha was there. "I don't know about sad, but he's a little nervous about the nanny he hired. I think she's going to be great. Quincy is just worried about the unknown."

She sighed. She was going to be the saddest over leaving Evie. The last two weeks had flown by. Looking after the eighteen-month-old was tiring but rewarding work.

Sorcha took Evie for a long, leisurely walk every day. Quincy's house was a quarter mile off the main road into town, so it was an easy walk, with sidewalks the rest of the way into town. Quincy's road was only used by him and one other neighbor, so she didn't have to worry about walking in the street with the stroller.

When she found out that Quincy had a library card, she asked to borrow it and took Evie every day to pick out new books to read.

The child loved being read to. Sorcha would sit in the rocker with her and read three or four books a day, as many as they could, while Evie took a bottle before lying down for her afternoon nap.

"I bet he wishes you lived here." Rosalie floated by and reached out to give Evie a pat on the arm. The child babbled at her.

Sorcha smiled at Evie's babbling. "Maybe. Days like today, I wish I lived here, too. I'm going to miss this."

"And we'll miss you," Rosalie said. "You come back when?"

"I'll be back on Wednesday. Linda's wedding is on Saturday, and then I'm scheduled to return home. I need to look for a new apartment and a new job. Back to the grind."

"If you need both those things, then you could move here." Rosalie playfully splashed water towards Evie as she floated by. "Find a job here. Or continue babysitting for Quincy."

"He can't afford health insurance for me, so there's that."

"My grandson Rob has one of those Internet jobs," Rosalie said. "He works from home all the time. Doesn't have to go to an office. He can work anywhere. You should do that."

"Hard to teach third graders remotely. COVID proved that."

The splashing of Rosalie's foot sent water over Sorcha's head, and a few drops hit Evie's face. She jerkily rubbed her hand over her eyes and pouted.

"You're OK, baby," Sorcha murmured as Winne harrumphed. Sorcha spun quickly, and Evie giggled.

"Who says you have to teach third graders? Maybe some adults need learnin'."

"Lots of adults need learnin'." Sorcha laughed. "But I don't know what I would teach them."

"Surely there are online courses that you could teach," Rosalie said, floating by. "Maybe for an online university or corporations. I had a job in the nineties teaching leadership courses for a company that catered to other companies. They've likely gone digital."

"Hmm, I hadn't thought about corporate trainers. You might be onto something there, Rosalie."

"And if you got something like that, you could move here. Forget finding a new roommate back in Illen-noise."

Sorcha considered. She wasn't completely tied to Illinois, but it would be a lot to pick up and move to a new state. Besides, Quincy was a wanderer. He didn't plan to stay in Florida for much longer. Who was to say he'd even want her tagging along? And if she was working remotely, she couldn't babysit for him. Unless they had jobs working opposite hours, and how fun would that be? Passing each other as they handed off Evie-watching duties.

Besides, while he'd shown interest, it seemed impossible to get through his defenses. They'd shared a few passionate kisses, but a little alcohol and a little romantic ambiance had fueled a couple of those. She couldn't tell what his genuine feelings towards her were.

She'd have a better point of view of where her own heart was when she got home. Maybe the adorable little girl in front of her was tipping the scales in Quincy's favor, and once she was apart from both of them, she'd be able to tell what was real and what was a dream.

Sorcha was dozing on the couch when Quincy got home. Evie had been asleep in her crib for a couple of hours. An afternoon in the sun and water had worn them out.

She heard the door open and sat up quickly, rubbing her eyes. The magazine she'd been reading when she fell asleep slipped to the floor.

Quincy stepped in, looking like he'd spent all evening throwing drunks out of the bar. Frown lines streaked across his forehead, and his eyes were shooting pistols.

"Why the hell have you not answered your phone?" he said, holding the door open like he intended to stand there until she walked out.

Sorcha blew out a breath. "Battery's dead, and I forgot the charger."

"All. Day?" It sounded like wires held his jaw together.

"Yes." She stood. "We were in the pool most of the afternoon, so I couldn't have answered, anyway."

"The pool?" Quincy glanced down. It was like saying the word made him register the toddler float that Sorcha had placed by the door after it dried. It took too much breath to fill the thing to deflate it after only one day. Once she told Quincy how much Evie loved the water, she was sure he'd want to take her all the time. Maybe he would even allow Ramona to take her swimming.

"Yes, we went to the Mockingbird and swam. Evie loved it. She especially loves Rosalie. Remember Rosalie and Winnie from the bar? They hung out with us."

Sorcha glanced at the clock on the wall. She had to be at the airport in fourteen hours and still needed to pack and sleep.

"Sorcha, you can't take my daughter out gallivanting around and not let me know where you are, especially if I can't get ahold of you. It's irresponsible. I've been worried."

"You've never called me or texted me while I was with Evie before. Why did you today? Slow night?" This was not her fault. He was being too hard-headed.

"She's my daughter. I can check up on her whenever I want."

"Look, I get it. I agree. Sorry, my phone wasn't working. But this seems like an overreaction. What gives?"

He finally closed the door, walked to the recliner, and sat down. Exhaustion and worry seemed to have taken its toll.

He leaned forward with his elbows propped on his knees and rested his head in his hands. It appeared as though a liquid had sloshed down his leg; either it was still wet, or something had left a stain.

Shaking his head, he looked up. "It doesn't matter. I should be able to get in touch with the sitter whenever I need to." He looked over at the pool float. "You took her swimming? That's dangerous. You shouldn't have done that without talking to me."

"Are you being serious right now? I'm a certified lifeguard. I'm a strong swimmer, and I know CPR. Besides, you live in Florida, next to the beach. She's going to need to learn."

"For now, she needs a trustworthy person watching her."

Sorcha scoffed. "You don't think I'm trustworthy? Look, I'm tired, you appear to be tired, and I'm getting on a plane tomorrow, with packing still to do. I'm going."

She grabbed her tote bag and threw it on her shoulder.

He laughed in a humorless, dismissive tone. "Of course, you still need to pack. You probably always wait until the last minute because you're impulsive. You lack planning and discipline."

Sorcha shook her head and walked out the door.

What was his problem? He was being unreasonable. She would have been packed (mostly) already if she hadn't been babysitting his kid for the last six days!

She growled as she crossed through the trees and shrubs separating his street from the beach. Hitting the sand, she pulled off her flip flops. She walked to the water's edge and turned south. Luckily, it was less than a mile to the Mockingbird walking along the beach.

His behavior was not acceptable. He'd probably just been on his best behavior while he needed her. Now that he had a nanny starting on Monday, and Sorcha was leaving, his true self was being exposed.

She should have known better than to get involved with him. It was supposed to be a vacation fling, but the dream of dating Quincy and having a simple fling flew out the window once his daughter arrived.

Winnie's words from earlier in the day came back to her. She had considered finding a job where she could be remote. If things were looking more promising with Quincy, she would have been all over it.

But the side of him she saw tonight was not appealing. Everyone was on their best behavior when you first got to know them. Most of the men she'd dated had eventually shown their true selves, and they usually fell short of her image of them.

She'd hoped Quincy was different. She was looking for gold under the gruff exterior. Maybe it wasn't there, after all.

The breeze was chilly, and she wished she'd thrown a jacket in her tote bag. The cold, damp air was settling into her bones. She wanted nothing more than to get back to the condo and crawl into bed, but she had to pack. At least by this time tomorrow night, she'd be home and ready to crawl into her own bed under her favorite blanket.

Chapter 21

A loud knock on the door jolted Sorcha's head up from where she was pulling food out of the refrigerator, deciding what needed to be tossed, shared with the building manager, or saved for Linda's family visit the following week.

Did Meridian come up to get the food? I told her I'd bring it down.

Sorcha walked to the door and flung it open. It wasn't Meridian. It was Quincy and Evie. They wore matching blue T-shirts and black shorts. Sorcha wanted to squeeze both of them.

Quincy held out a bag. "I brought donuts to apologize for my shi—icky behavior last night."

Sorcha smiled at Evie but crossed her arms and squinted her eyes at Quincy. "If you think a few donuts will win me over...you're right! Come on in."

Quincy glanced around the condo. Her large suitcase was sitting next to the door and a carry-on was open on the couch so she could toss in the miscellaneous stuff she found while tidying up.

"Nice place," he said, entering. "Is it safe to put Evie down?"

"Yes, but there aren't any toys here."

"That's okay. I came prepared." He set the bag of donuts on the counter, put Evie down, and pulled a backpack off his shoulder. He pulled out three baby dolls and put them on the ottoman for Evie.

"Want a cup of coffee? I can make a small pot."

"If you don't mind. Yes."

Sorcha filled the coffeemaker with grounds, added water, and turned the machine on. "You two are up early today."

"She leaves me no choice."

Sorcha watched Evie rearrange the dolls on the ottoman, then grabbed paper towels for the donuts; she didn't want to wash more dishes than necessary. The clock on the microwave reminded her she had to leave for the airport in ninety minutes.

"Look," Quincy began. "I want to apologize for my attitude last night. Being stressed out was no excuse for acting like I did. I'm sorry."

Sorcha sighed. "I'll accept your apology and add my own; you were right; I should have been reachable. That's not an unreasonable request. It hurt me when you called me irresponsible. I feel like my responsibility meter is turned all the way up when I'm with children, whether that's my classroom or with Evie."

"Thank you for that. It's good that we're communicating."

"Agree. Like healthy adults."

"Never thought I'd be called that." Quincy stepped closer. "Hug it out?"

"Yes, sir!"

She embraced him and closed her eyes. He squeezed her gently, and she wanted more. More time like this, in Quincy's arms.

Evie let out a squeal and came trotting over. Sorcha looked down, and Evie tapped Sorcha's leg. "Me," she cried, hands up in the air.

Quincy laughed. "Someone is feeling left out." He reached down and pulled Evie up, but instead of stepping away from Sorcha like she feared, he put Evie on his hip and pulled Sorcha in for a group hug.

This! Much more of this.

Evie giggled as she leaned into Sorcha, who turned and gave the toddler a kiss on her cheek. "Hey, Evie, sweetie. I'm going to miss you."

"The feeling is shared," Quincy said.

"I'll be back on Wednesday."

"And busy."

"Well, that's true. But I'm sure I'll see you. I know where you work, after all."

The coffee pot made the gurgling sound that meant it was ready for consumption.

"Coffee and donuts?" Sorcha asked.

"No coffee for Evie, but yes." Quincy pulled back from the group hug.

As Sorcha grabbed two coffee mugs out of the cabinet, Quincy put Evie back in front of the dolls. He walked to the wall of sliding patio doors and looked out at the incredible view of the Gulf.

"Wow. Amazing view," he said.

"I know. Incredible. That balcony is one of the best places in the whole country. It will set you right when you're freaked out about something."

Quincy laughed, a deep, soft sound. Sorcha wanted to record the sound so she could listen to it at home.

"And what do you freak out about?" he asked.

"Life. Am I making good choices? Where should my career go? How do we solve poverty in this country?"

"Minor things."

The sarcasm was funny. Quincy rarely expressed sarcasm. If he didn't agree with something, he'd typically ignore it.

"It's all relative." Sorcha opened the bag of donuts. "Which donut is yours?"

"Ladies get first pick."

"No. I bet there is one in here you're hoping for."

"All right. The maple glaze is my favorite."
"Then it's yours. I like the chocolate sprinkle one. Anything for Evie?"
"I'm keeping her from sweets for now. Unless she comes over and begs for a bite."
"Solid."
"What time do you have to leave for the airport?"
"Two. I'll call a rideshare at one-thirty."
"We can give you a ride."
"It's kind of a long drive."
"I'm sure Evie will take a nice nap. I don't mind."
"If you insist."
"I do."

They sat at the kitchen island drinking coffee and eating donuts. Quincy asked her about job hunting, and she filled him in on the latest prospects. She had two interviews lined up for the few days she'd be home.

Of course, she didn't want those jobs but was hoping the experience would be worth the time. She'd been with her school for seven years. It had been a long time since she'd interviewed.

She'd also found a very interesting corporate training position that was one hundred percent remote. The job was to conduct online new hire and other human resource training for a large retail chain. But she didn't mention this, or any remote job, to Quincy. He'd probably run for the door if he had an inkling he and Evie were a consideration in her search.

Sorcha thought it was an interesting opportunity, and she liked the idea of a remote position. She could see herself becoming one of those camper-van nomads that traveled all over the U.S. seeing the scenery, making memories, and meeting new people.

When she was a kid, her family didn't take vacations involving long car drives. They mostly visited family. Her dad had grown up in Michigan, and his brother had a lake house there. The few times they took a real vacation, they flew.

The idea of road-trip vacations appealed to her. She loved watching content creators who filled the #vanlife feeds. It seemed magical to take your home with you wherever you wanted to go, within reason. The biggest challenge she saw to the idea was downsizing her clothes and accessories to the essentials. But she'd figure it out.

Then there was the loneliness challenge. One thing she'd learned about herself on this vacation was that she wasn't cut out for extended periods on her own.

She could get a cat for company and leash-train it. She hoped it would sleep on the dashboard as she drove. Once Linda moved out of their apartment, she'd take her cats with her, and Sorcha was determined to get her own. She just needed to get the traveling kind of cat; then she'd be set.

Maybe someday she'd have a partner, too.

Chapter 22

As soon as Sorcha got home, she dropped her bags by the front door and dropped on the couch to snuggle with Linda's cats, Missy and Buddy.

Linda was updating Sorcha on the goings-on at her retail stationery boutique.

"Good to hear you've been busy at the store," Sorcha said, scratching behind Buddy's ear.

"It is!" Linda plopped into the nearby easy chair and picked up a feather toy to play with the cats. "I thought once summer hit and college kids left town it would slow down, but it's been steady. Guess those online ads I'm running are working."

"I'm glad you got help with them. I've heard they can be tricky."

"Certainly. All right, now that you're home, I want to hear all about your time with Quincy. Seems like you were with him *a lot*."

Sorcha sighed. "I've spent oodles more hours with his daughter than him."

"Did he pay you for babysitting?"

"No." Sorcha shook her head. "He offered, but I wouldn't take any money for it. He was in a jam. I had the time and was bored, honestly. Don't let me go on a solo vacation ever again. Unless I have a fantastic reason."

Linda laughed. The joyful sound filled Sorcha's emotional piggy bank. It was good to be home. She was going to miss these days casually hanging with her best friend and roommate.

"Fine. But you're deflecting. We should talk about Quincy. Now that you've gotten to know him better, tell me things."

Sorcha took a breath. Where to start? "Quincy's complicated. Stubborn. Like he decided sometime in the past that he was no good with women, so he wouldn't date ever again..."

Linda interjected, "Never say never."

"I know! Good motto! Anyway, I finally dragged him out of that comfort zone a teeny, tiny bit. Got him to take me for a motorcycle ride. Then when he found out about his daughter, he saw me as a convenient helper. I think he would have drowned without my support."

"Was he appreciative?"

"Yes." Sorcha thought of all the treats he'd brought. "And then, there were a few sparks..."

"Yes?" Linda wiggled her eyebrows. "Now we're getting to the good stuff."

"Sparks, but little fire. Can't blame him; he's now responsible for this little human. It's a lot. I couldn't distract him from that."

"But you want to distract him?"

"Yes! Maybe it's not rational, but I could fall for him. He's quiet, which you wouldn't think I would like, but I do, and he's quick-witted. And this will melt your heart; he takes care of stray animals!"

Linda let out a soft, "Aw."

"Plus, he's so good with his daughter. And he didn't get any time to prepare for that. Talk about trial by fire!"

Linda nodded.

"Some men might not even have said yes if they found out like that." The cat jumped down from her lap. Guess he didn't miss her that much. "But Quincy did. He's solid. Responsible."

"How did you leave things with him? Did it just end?" Linda asked.

"No. We had a rough spot on Friday night. We both said some things when we were tired." She hated confessing to this next part. "I messed up. I let my phone die when I was babysitting, and he couldn't get hold of me. He was mad. But he came to the condo before I left this morning to apologize. And he brought donuts. Actually, he provided a different treat every day this week. I'm feeling spoiled."

His visit told her, even if he didn't say it, that he cared. Theirs was not just a business relationship. There was more to it. Yes, he still battled the idea of a relationship, but she wasn't giving up on him yet.

Linda leaned forward with a smile. "That's sweet! You deserve to be spoiled. Do you think he'll come to the wedding?"

"Maybe?" Sorcha shrugged. He hadn't committed.

Sorcha tapped her foot. Buddy ran over to her and bit her shoelaces. They were bright pink with sparkles. How could a cat resist?

"Hmm." Linda frowned and clicked her tongue. "Seems like you have more questions than answers about him."

"Seems so. We'll see what happens. But let's not focus on Quincy. Let's talk about your wedding! Are you nervous? Excited?"

"Both! And so much more. I'm glad we're having a small, casual wedding. I would be nervous if it was an extravagant affair."

"It will be beautiful. Meridian got the package you sent her."

"Good. Oh, I was talking to Mason today, and he told me they've posted several new administrative positions at his hospital. One is a communications—"

"Nope! I'll stop you there. You know I can't do hospitals. No way, no how."

"Oh, that's right." Linda made a scrunched-up face. "Sorry, I forgot. We were talking about your job search, and he mentioned those. I didn't think about your 'aversion.'"

Sorcha nodded. "That's a nice way to say fear and dislike. I'll have to remember aversion."

Linda's phone rang, and she groaned. "Ugh. It's my sister. She's coming over to drop off the 'something borrowed'. She texted when she left her house. You know, talking to her when she's driving is like talking to an alien that's just landed on earth. She tells me about *everything* she sees as she's passing."

Sorcha laughed. "Enjoy that. I'm going to unpack."

Sorcha dragged her bags to her room. She unpacked and filled her laundry basket. She'd go to the laundromat first thing in the morning.

Putting her clean clothes away, she saw the dress she'd wear at Linda's wedding. It was a simple sheath dress, pale lavender, with a dark lavender sash. The shoulder straps were strings of lavender crystals. She felt so fancy and romantic wearing it. She wished Quincy would see her in the dress. If he didn't come to the wedding (he hadn't committed, but he hadn't said no either!), she just might stomp down to his bar, or his house, wherever he was, to show him.

Chapter 23

"*Hasta luego*, Ramona," Quincy said, raising a hand to say good night to the new nanny. She said goodbye three times before reaching her compact car at the curb.

Sorcha had been correct. Ramona was the best of the group they'd interviewed. Not only had she watched Evie, but she had also cleaned every inch of the small house. He was going to pay her extra for the bonus labor.

She'd given him a full written report of everything Evie had done or said while Quincy was gone. He smiled to see Ramona's notes about diaper discoveries, a tally of how many times Evie said "DaDa" (fifteen), and Evie's preference for the pink bunny blanket over the plain white one.

There had been no phone calls or text messages while he'd been at work. And when he got home, Evie was sound asleep in her crib.

Ramona had been mopping the kitchen floor when he walked in, so he was waiting for it to dry before grabbing the bag of potato chips and a container of ranch dip for a bedtime snack.

Work had been steady, surprising for a Monday night, which was good, because if it had been slow he would have had too much time to worry about Evie with the sitter.

Even with the pace of this shift, he'd wished Sorcha was sitting at the bar, talking and flirting with him.

It had only been two days since she'd gone, but it felt like weeks. She had become an important part of his life in such a short time.

Pulling his boots off, he decided the floor was dry enough. He needed that snack.

Opening the fridge for the dip, he smiled in disbelief to see that Ramona had cooked a small pot roast. There was a covered plate on the top shelf containing beef, potatoes, carrots, and mushrooms.

His stomach growled as he reached for the dish. "Ramona, you are a rockstar," he mumbled, ripping the plastic wrap off the plate and sliding it into the microwave.

How have I gone from not wanting or needing a woman in my life to having two incredible women and one amazing little girl in it?

Wondering what Sorcha was doing, he glanced at his watch. Eleven o'clock. It would only be ten in Illinois. She might still be awake.

Was she missing him or regretting the time she'd spent with him? She would be back in just two days, and he couldn't wait to see her.

He was still debating going to the wedding with her. Just in case he did, he'd asked for the day off and had to switch his shift with Jasmyn, but it was arranged. He would wait to see how things went with Sorcha when she returned.

Likely, he had just been a vacation interest to Sorcha. Once she got home, got back in her own world, she'd remember that he wasn't the type of guy for her.

Placing the warmed plate on the table, he picked up his phone and sent her a quick text.

QUINCY: You up?

He took a bite of the roast and sighed. It was delicious.

SORCHA: Are you kidding? I'm just getting started!

He smiled. That sounded right.

> **QUINCY**: Out on the town?

SORCHA: Sadly, no. I've got my PJs on, hair in a pony, face mask on, and I'm applying to a bunch of jobs online.

> **QUINCY**: You know how to live.

SORCHA: How was the first day with Ramona?

> **QUINCY**: Great.

He snapped a picture of his meal and sent it to her with the words, "She cooks!"

SORCHA: Fantastic. I hope Evie didn't eat too much of that beef.

> **QUINCY**: According to the very detailed notes Ramona left, Evie had exactly 2.5 ounces of beef and three carrots.

SORCHA: That is detailed. Hey, want to call me when you're done eating? I'd love to hear your voice.

> **QUINCY**: You've forgotten what I sound like already?

SORCHA: Well, I was trying to remember if you sounded more like Harry Styles or Ed Sheeran.

> **QUINCY**: Who?

> **SORCHA**: Never mind. Just call me. PRETTY PLEASE!

After eating and washing his dishes, he grabbed a beer from the fridge and walked to the couch to sit, moving the two baby dolls that were occupying his preferred side. From this angle, he could look out his front door. There was enough moonlight that he could see the outline of the bushes that flanked his porch. The windows in the front were open and a light breeze fluttered the blinds, a pull cord bouncing against the windowsill.

Propping his feet up on the coffee table, he pushed the call button on his phone and leaned back. Anticipating hearing Sorcha's voice put a smile on his face.

"Well, hello, you," she said.

"Hi, yourself."

"How'd you do today, Dad? Able to work without worrying about Evie?"

"It was busy enough, so yes, I didn't worry." He waited for a beat. "Too much."

"Ah, that's good. Was Evie awake when you got home?"

"No. Ramona's note said Evie fussed at her for a few minutes while she put her pajamas on but went to bed when Ramona offered to read."

"Aw, that's great. See, I told you Ramona was the one."

Quincy thought about "the one". There was only one person who came to mind. Sorcha.

"That you did. How was your flight home?"

"Groovy. No issues. It's a whirlwind here now with the last-minute prep for Lindy Lu's wedding. Can't believe I'll be back there on Wednesday."

Quincy couldn't believe it, either. But he wasn't taking anything for granted. "How long are you staying this time?"

"Just until Sunday. Their condo is full, so I'm staying at the B&B on Coconut Cove. I can't afford to stay there for very long. It's pricey."

"That place is close to the bar."

"I know."

He could hear the smile in her voice. She was as pleased as he was that it was close. Maybe he could get off his shift a little early and stop by before going home. He'd love to see Sorcha alone.

They were silent for several moments. Quincy felt his chest squeeze. Was Sorcha thinking about the possibility of having some alone time?

"So," Sorcha continued, breaking into his thoughts, "have you decided if you'll come to the wedding?"

He'd given it a lot of thought but still hadn't decided. Things were more complicated with Evie.

"If I do, I'll have Evie."

"That's fine!" Sorcha's voice was excited. "OOOH! I can go shopping to find a dress for her."

"No, don't," he protested.

"Hey, don't fight me on this. I want to. I love to shop."

"Yes, you do. Fine. And yes, we'll go."

"You will? Great! The wedding is at six. Just come around five thirty. There will be a few chairs, but the service will be quick. You could just stand."

Quincy chuckled. "I'll probably be chasing Evie, making sure she doesn't eat sand."

"Right. I wish I could be with you to help get Evie ready. Pretty dress, pretty hairdo." She sighed. "Well, at least after the ceremony, I can help you keep an eye on her."

"No. It's your best friend's wedding. You need to have fun. But I would like to see you dressed up all fancy."

"You would?"

"Of course I would."

He'd want a picture, too, so he could have that memory long after she tired of him and moved on with her life.

"Well, if you come, you will. OK, I need to wash this face mask off. I can hardly move my mouth."

"Ha. Night, Sorcha."

"Good night, Quincy. See you soon."

He hung up the phone and tossed it on the couch. She was going to be the best and the worst thing that had ever happened to him; he could feel it in his soul. Sorcha had already left an indelible mark on him. He felt himself changing for the better because of her.

Somehow, Sorcha had broken through the shield he'd held up for so long. Once she came to her senses and left, he would reinforce his boundaries and not let another one in. He owed that much to Evie, and to himself.

Evie would have enough challenges in life without her mom. He wouldn't add to her burdens by parading women in and out of their lives.

To be the best dad for his daughter, he needed to be strong. Available to his daughter and focused on her one hundred percent. He wouldn't let his mistakes damage Evie.

His biggest question was, would Sorcha be another mistake? He hoped not.

Chapter 24

Exhausted, Sorcha flopped onto her back on the double bed with three comforters piled atop it.

The Bird of Paradise Inn was a quaint B&B two blocks east of the Mockingbird. She was thankful she'd booked the room months ago. The closest hotel was twenty minutes away, and she wanted to be close to the wedding shenanigans. And Quincy.

When she checked into the bed-and-breakfast, the owner showed her a laminated sheet of paper with pictures of five Florida birds. Sorcha had to pick a bird to choose her room. No picture of the room or list of its amenities, just a picture of a bird. The owner of the B&B explained that each room had a bird theme.

So Sorcha picked the Painted Bunting room. When she entered the room she found paintings on the walls depicting the red-chested bird. And there was a lifelike stuffed bird perched on a small piece of driftwood on the dresser. Sorcha hoped it had been created at the hands of a skilled artisan and was not a taxidermy specimen.

From her position on the bed, the bird seemed to watch her, so she jumped up and tossed the doily from the nightstand over the bird's head.

Her movement reminded her of how tired she was. After the early morning flight, and a long day spent assembling the wedding favors—an adorable assortment of notepads and notebooks which Linda had designed herself—Sorcha was exhausted.

Linda and Mason planned an elaborate scavenger hunt for Thursday as a wedding-guest mixer, and Friday was reserved for any last-minute issues and the rehearsal on the beach before the fireworks.

She was starting to doubt she would see Quincy before the ceremony. Each hour seemed to be filled with preparations and parties. Normally, the activities would thrill her, but she yearned to have time with Quincy and Evie on this trip.

She was continuing to receive responses to her job applications, and she hoped to line up even more interviews starting the following week when she was back home and could concentrate on the job search in earnest.

Though she still questioned her next move, she was confident that it was going to work out.

Her phone beeped, and she groaned as she reached for it. She needed to clean up, pull all the comforters off the bed, shove them in the closet, and crawl under the sheets.

> **QUINCY:** I'm sorry. We're slammed tonight, a lot of out-of-town guests, I hear, and I can't leave early.

Sorcha sighed in relief. She wanted to see Quincy, and if he'd said he was coming, she would be ecstatic, but if he couldn't come, she could get some much-needed sleep.

> **SORCHA:** Oh, bummer. Maybe tmrw?

She hoped he'd understand the abbreviation; he didn't seem to be the kind to text frequently.

> **QUINCY:** I hope so. Night, Sorcha.

She replied with a yawn emoji.

Stumbling into the private en suite, she looked at the mascara that had flaked and given her shadows under her eyes. *Darn humidity! Add a trip to get waterproof mascara tomorrow to the list.*

She had to see Quincy before the wedding; she needed to give him the dress for Evie. It had taken her three hours and seven store visits on Tuesday to find a frilly dress for Evie in the same lavender shade as Sorcha's bridesmaid dress. Evie's dress was topped by an adorable white sweater with purple rosebuds for buttons.

Sorcha hoped people wouldn't look at the dress and make assumptions about her relationship with Quincy and Evie. It wasn't wrong to coordinate outfits with wedding guests. It wasn't wrong to want to buy Quincy's daughter a dress.

But it felt a little funny.

She wasn't trying to jump in and be a stepmom to Evie. She wasn't sure how Quincy truly felt about her. He was kind and attentive, and he seemed attracted to her. The few kisses they'd shared were the absolute best she'd ever had.

No other boyfriend could come close to causing the warmth and giddiness in her body that Quincy did.

He was everything she hadn't known she wanted. And since none of her prior boyfriends had worked out, that must be a good thing.

She still couldn't imagine everything working out for the two of them. The physical distance was the first and largest obstacle.

But she'd put in a few applications for jobs in Texas, where Quincy said he was thinking about moving next in his journey around the U.S. It was a long shot, but she enjoyed taking those shots.

It was going to be difficult, with this weekend's focus being on Linda and Mason's wedding, but she needed to have a meaningful conversation with Quincy about what was possible. Was she exaggerating his feelings for her? Did they have a fighting chance? She was going to find out.

Crawling into bed, she imagined Evie in the pretty dress and the shiny white Mary Jane shoes that she'd bought. She had to get a picture of Evie in the dress, perhaps even a picture of the two of them together.

Even better, a picture of the three of them together.

Sorcha bounced on her toes. Maybe she'd had one too many espressos, but it was a jam-packed day, and she needed the caffeine reserves to keep up with the bride-to-be and all the pre-wedding activities.

She knocked again, hoping Evie wasn't sleeping.

A few seconds later Quincy opened the door, Evie on his hip.

"We hoped that was you," he said.

Evie squealed and held out her hands to Sorcha. Sorcha put the small dress bag over the chair on Quincy's porch and held out her hands to Evie, who launched herself off Quincy into Sorcha's waiting arms.

"Hi, Evie, sweetie!" Sorcha said. "I missed you!"

"We missed you. Come in. I'll get your bags." Quincy held the door wide, and Sorcha stepped inside.

She noticed the hum of the window air conditioner. "That's new," she said, tilting her head towards the unit.

"It's one thing for me to be grouchy in the heat. It's a whole other thing for her," he said with a smile.

"I bet." Sorcha swung Evie side to side, enjoying the weight and warmth of the child.

Too soon, Evie pointed. "Down," she said in her sweet, soft voice.

"Of course, girlie." Sorcha gave her a quick kiss and placed her on the floor.

Quincy stepped closer. "Do I get one of those?"

Sorcha beamed as she turned towards him. "Miss me?"

"You have no idea."

She stepped closer and touched his beard, its coarse hairs tickling her palm. "I missed this."

"Is that all?"

"And this." She leaned up and kissed him.

Yes, this she had missed. It had only been five days, but it felt much longer.

Quincy smelled like the beach, warm, salty, and fresh. He put his arms around her and pulled her closer, tilting his head to maintain the kiss.

Her arms went around his neck, leaning into him.

A moment later, she felt Evie's hand on her leg, tapping her. Sorcha moaned softly and pulled away from Quincy.

"Yes, Evie?" she asked, looking down at the girl who was holding a baby doll.

"Bay. Bee," she said.

"Yes," Sorcha chuckled. "Baby. Hey, do you want to see the dress?"

Quincy squinted his eyes. "It's a good thing she's so cute. Sure."

Sorcha laughed. "Yes, she's good at interrupting things."

Moving to where Quincy had put the dress bag on the couch, she unzipped the bag and pulled back the fabric. "I won't take it out, but here's the dress, and the shoes are at the bottom."

"Adorable," Quincy said in a deadpan voice.

"Hey, you like it, right?"

"I'm teasing. It's very cute. You just have to remember that I'm not used to the pastel colors and frilly details."

Sorcha looked him up and down. He wore his usual black T-shirt with black shorts. No shoes or socks. Not surprising in this heat, though the A/C was keeping the room nice and cool.

"Well, get used to the frills." Sorcha shook her head with a grin. "They're not going away anytime soon. Unfortunately, I need to go. Bridesmaid duties are calling. It was great that I could break away for a bit. I'll see you two at the rehearsal tomorrow. I can't wait to have some time to hang out with you."

"Looking forward to it." Quincy pulled her close and kissed her forehead.

Sorcha shut her eyes to mark the memory. She was going to need these wonderful moments to sustain her when she left again in just three days.

Chapter 25

Quincy drove to the Mockingbird, instead of walking, because Evie had so many necessary items. A change of clothes, diapers, food, beach toys, water, a towel in case he took her into the water, and several things he couldn't remember but knew she needed.

It was the fourth of July, and Sorcha told him that the rehearsal was at six, after which the wedding party would hang out on the beach to watch the fireworks.

She'd told him about these details on Thursday when she had ten minutes to stop and drop off the dress and shoes she'd bought Evie for the wedding.

He had to admit the dress was darling. Sorcha had that woman's touch that would be impossible for him to provide for Evie. He didn't know the first thing about dresses, or hair bows, or a thousand other girlie things.

The thought of raising a little girl on his own was terrifying. There were going to be so many things that he wouldn't understand how to handle as she grew up.

He'd never let her date, of course. Not until she was eighteen. He knew how boys were, and no boy was going to get close to his daughter until she was a legal, consenting adult.

These thoughts had made him seriously consider moving to Orlando to be close to his sister, who would give Evie the motherly figure she'd need whenever Quincy messed things up or was clueless.

Of course, there was the slim possibility that things with Sorcha would work out. It'd been a blow to his system when she said she didn't have time for him until tonight. She'd been in town for almost three days, and he'd only seen her briefly when she'd stopped by.

She'd visited just long enough to upset Evie when she left. The poor girl had let out a wail as Sorcha walked out the door. The sound echoed Quincy's own pain at seeing Sorcha leave.

But they would see her tonight. Soon. He grabbed the large tote bag and diaper-bag backpack from the trunk before extracting Evie from the backseat.

"Ready to play in the sand, baby girl?" he asked.

"Wata," she said, pointing to the Gulf.

"Yes, it is. We'll take off our shoes and get our toes wet. How does that sound?"

He hefted his daughter onto his hip, ensuring she didn't get tangled in the backpack straps. Lifting the tote off the ground, he started for the beach.

A small group gathered in a circle near the water. There were rows of chairs arranged in a semicircle, facing the water.

This must be the wedding party. He scanned the group for a sign of Sorcha. Spotting her, he pointed her out to Evie. "See Sorcha? The beautiful lady in the pink top and white shorts."

She was barefoot, and her hair was pulled back off her face, which made her look even younger. She was smiling and seemed to glow in the setting sun.

After setting every detail in his memory, he glanced at the man she was talking to. He was tall, slender but built like an athlete. His hair was full in the front, according to the trend, and he wore a pink polo shirt with cream shorts. Did they confer on their attire? Was this the best man?

It was easy to picture the two of them at their own wedding rehearsal. They looked made for each other, like two stars in a blockbuster Hollywood rom-com.

Sorcha and the man next to her were close in age, probably had similar suburban, middle-class backgrounds. He wouldn't come with the sort of messy baggage Quincy did.

He took a deep breath to shake the dark thoughts. He had to trust Sorcha's words and actions and not let his past guide his future.

Quincy didn't realize he'd stopped short and stared until Evie tugged on his T-shirt. Black, as usual. He'd found the one pair of board shorts he owned, dark gray, and wore his recently purchased sports slides.

How would he approach Sorcha? She was with her friends, ready to celebrate a wedding. He couldn't walk up to her and kiss her like he wanted to.

Maybe he'd wait for her to notice him. He walked about thirty feet from the wedding group and set the tote bag and backpack on the ground before pulling Evie's shoes off and letting her down.

"Stay by me," he said as he reached into the tote bag. He pulled out the beach blanket and a plastic bucket with a sand scoop, which he handed to his daughter.

He kept stealing glances at Sorcha as he got out the play things for Evie. Once the toddler was sitting, happily filling the bucket, then kicking it over to start again, he pulled the small soft-sided cooler out of the tote and grabbed a bottle of water.

He slid it into a koozie and sat on the blanket. Looking out at the water, he took a few deep breaths.

"Da," Evie said, growing bored with the sand.

"Yes, Evie-girl?"

"Da, wata, Da."

He chuckled. "Yes, let's do that."

He finished the water, put the empty bottle back into the cooler, and removed his shoes. Taking up Evie's hand, he led her to the water, enjoying the sound of her laughter as the waves hit her feet and lower legs.

They played in the water, laughing and splashing, for about fifteen minutes before Quincy glanced back towards the wedding rehearsal party. Just as he found Sorcha again, her face turned towards him, and he saw the moment she recognized him.

She smiled broadly and threw her hand in the air to wave. He tilted his head back in acknowledgment. His hands were holding both of Evie's, ensuring she didn't get knocked over by a wave.

Sorcha said something to the handsome man next to her, resting her hand on his arm. They both laughed, and Quincy felt his throat tighten.

Evie babbled excitedly, and he looked down to see if she had noticed Sorcha. She hadn't. She watched a small shell tumbling in the sand.

"Yikes!" He lifted Evie in the air just before her foot landed on the shell. "That was close."

He glanced up to see Sorcha walking briskly towards them. "Hello!" she called when she was still twenty feet away.

"So-So!" Evie called, recognizing her.

"Aw, sweet angel! Are you having fun?" Sorcha rushed the last few steps and tripped in the sand, splaying forward.

"Fu-udgecicle!" Quincy called. He shook his head at his creative swear. Having Evie around, he was finding new, kid-friendly terms.

Sorcha slid to a stop in a move that would have impressed a major-league baseball coach, and Quincy teasingly called, "You're safe!"

Sorcha looked up, laughter in her eyes and sand on her chin. "Thanks, Ump."

"Are you all right?" he asked as Evie tried to pull free of his hands to get to Sorcha.

"Nothing hurt but my pride." Sorcha stood and ran her hands down her chest, knocking sand off her shirt and shorts. "I'll need to go in and change my clothes. Luckily, I brought another outfit for tonight."

Having cleaned herself off, she kneeled and held her arms out for Evie. "Hey, Evie sweetie!"

The little girl broke free of Quincy's grasp and rushed to Sorcha, who swept her up in a big hug.

"I'm so glad to see you guys. We finished the rehearsal and are going in for dinner. Want to join us?"

"No, we ate before we came. Evie might get restless if I pull her out of the sand too soon."

"Oh," Sorcha's face fell. "Well, after dinner, we're coming back out. The building is going to have a big bonfire as we wait for the fireworks. You can meet everyone then."

Quincy thought about the man he'd seen with Sorcha. He didn't want to meet everyone. "Maybe. We're not staying for the fireworks."

He'd planned to stay for the fireworks, but not now. He was clearly interrupting Sorcha's fun with her friends. She didn't need him and Evie distracting her.

"You're not?" Her eyebrows knitted together.

"I'm not sure Evie will react well to the noise. I wanted to get some ear protection and didn't have time."

That was a little white lie; he had earmuffs in the tote bag. But it made a good excuse not to stay.

Sorcha didn't need them to weigh her down. She was young and needed to be there to support her friend, have fun, and live her life. She didn't need two anchors around her neck.

"Oh. I understand. I could see if someone here has ear protection." Her voice was optimistic. There was nothing that could hold her back; she'd always get what she wanted.

That was an admirable trait. One he would have loved to have in his life; her enthusiasm was a good balance to his cynicism. It would be good for Evie to have that in her life, too.

"No, don't bother. We're going to hang out here. I'll teach Evie what sandcastles are. I'll wait until she's worn out, then we'll head home."

"All right. Well, you're coming to the wedding tomorrow, and I'll spend lots of time with both of you then! I can't believe I have to go home on Sunday. This trip has been too short."

"That's because you extended your first trip to help me with Evie. You can't move here permanently." Quincy laughed, but Sorcha didn't seem to see the humor in his statement.

"Right." She put Evie down, and Quincy took his daughter's hand. "Well, I'm going to clean up before dinner." She leaned forward and kissed Quincy on the cheek.

He felt the dampness on her face from where she'd fallen in the surf. "Hold on." He leaned back and studied her face, brushing a small clump of sand from her neck. "Get that shower."

Sorcha laughed. "Right. See you guys tomorrow!" She bent down and kissed Evie's cheek.

Tomorrow. They'd have tomorrow, and that was it. After watching her best friend get married, starting a life with her partner, planning their own family, Sorcha would probably realize that's what she wanted, too. The fairy-tale romance. The hero to sweep her off her feet. Not the old guy trying to figure out how to be a dad to an eighteen-month-old.

Life was all about adjusting. Adjusting to the disappointments and the opportunities. Smiling when your heart was breaking and cursing creatively when kids were around.

Quincy had been through this before. He had survived, and he'd survive again.

It was just that this time, he'd let himself feel the hope that seemed to spring from Sorcha like the mythical fountain of youth, full of life, laughter, and a pinch of magic.

Chapter 26

The wedding ceremony lasted ten very emotional minutes, as Linda and Mason pledged their love and fidelity to each other before God and the guests.

Sorcha held a small handkerchief wrapped around the bouquet of pink and lavender flowers that Linda had crafted out of thin pieces of wood. Thank goodness for the hankie, because Sorcha's tears began flowing as soon as Linda told Mason in her shaking voice how he was her soul's sanctuary, and how once they'd reconnected, she had never felt so loved and cherished.

As the preacher pronounced Linda and Mason husband and wife, Evie yelled, "Yay!" in her sweet child's voice and everyone laughed.

Sorcha worried Linda might be upset at the interruption, but when she threw her head back and laughed, Sorcha knew it was fine. She glanced over to where Quincy sat with Evie standing on his lap.

Quincy wore a black button-down dress shirt with dark gray trousers. Evie looked adorable in her dress and sweater. Sorcha smiled when she saw the purple bows in Evie's hair; she wondered how long it had taken Quincy to fix them, or if he'd had help.

Linda and Mason kissed, and the guests cheered. As they turned to walk down the aisle, Sorcha leaned down to straighten Linda's train and shook off the sand that covered the fabric.

The wedding party and guests proceeded into the building. There would be a dinner in the large community room on the first floor of the Mockingbird.

Sorcha was excited about introducing Linda to Evie, especially after Evie's enthusiastic reaction during the ceremony.

When Quincy and Evie entered, Sorcha beamed. She'd worried that Quincy wouldn't come in for the dinner, finding some excuse to avoid meeting her friends.

She hurried over and picked Evie up in a hug. Evie squealed and clasped Sorcha's neck.

"You look so beautiful, Evie-girl," she crooned. Looking at Quincy, she added, "You're pretty handsome yourself, Mr. Q."

"Guess I clean up all right."

"Come. I want you to meet Linda and Mason right away."

She grabbed Quincy's hand and pulled, still carrying Evie. Evie shifted, and Sorcha had to drop Quincy's hand to pull her thin strap back onto her shoulder.

Linda clapped as the trio approached. "Hi, Quincy! This must be your daughter. I've heard so much about you, little one. Nice to meet you."

Linda held out her hand, and Evie tentatively reached out with her own. Linda clasped her hand and gave it a quick kiss.

Evie smiled and said, "Pur-te," pointing at Linda.

"Yes, she is, Evie," Sorcha said, bouncing the girl on her hip.

Linda sighed. "Ah, thank you." Turning to Quincy, she said, "Quincy, I'm not sure if you've officially met my *husband*, Mason," she trilled. "His family has had a condo here as long as mine has. He's probably been in Crabbie's a time or two."

"You look familiar," Quincy said, reaching out to shake hands with the groom and then the bride. "It was a beautiful ceremony. Thank you both for letting us attend."

"It was perfect," said Linda. "Everything we wanted and then some. I hope you'll stay for the bonfire later. It will be low key and fun."

"Two of my favorite things," Quincy said. "We'll stay as late as this little girl can keep her eyes open."

Sorcha reached into her small purse and pulled out her phone. "I hate to ask the bride to work on her wedding day, but would you please take a picture of the three of us?" She pointed to Quincy and Evie.

"Of course I will!" Linda said, reaching for the phone.

Quincy stepped next to Sorcha and put his hand on her lower back. Sorcha bounced Evie on her hip, asking the child to smile.

Once the picture was snapped, Sorcha sent it to Quincy when he asked.

Sorcha moved slowly in a circle, pointing out the decorations to Evie.

Linda and Mason moved off to greet more guests, and Quincy offered to take Evie. "She's going to wrinkle your gorgeous dress."

"For her, I don't mind." Sorcha handed Evie to her dad. "It's a casual dinner, no head table. We can sit anywhere. Want to grab some seats? Maybe over by that window?"

"Lead the way."

Sorcha stopped to remind Laurel, Linda's twin sister, that they were to give the DJ a few last-minute instructions in thirty minutes.

"A DJ?" Quincy asked when they sat down.

"Yes, Mason insisted. He wanted to ensure there was good music, good times, and good vibes all night. His words."

"Dancing on the beach. Interesting."

"Probably just swaying on the beach, but it will be nice. Romantic."

Quincy gave her a look. She wasn't sure how to interpret it. Did he mean romance was out of the question, or was he looking forward to it? It was hard to read him most of the time.

After they ate, Evie got antsy, and Quincy said they needed to leave.

"Oh, don't go now. The night is young,"

"And so is Evie, who has an eight o'clock bedtime."

"Darn it!" Sorcha cried. "We should have gotten a sitter for Evie so you could stay. Probably too late now, huh? Want to give Ramona a call?"

Quincy laughed and shook his head. "I'll not risk losing our amazing nanny by calling her at the last minute to babysit. Unless it was an actual emergency."

"This feels like an emergency." She pouted at Quincy with wide eyes, hoping her pathetic face would convince him to call the sitter.

Quincy just shook his head and leaned forward to kiss Sorcha on the nose. "We're going home. Say good night, Evie."

Evie matched Sorcha's pout. "Nite, So-So."

"Nite, Evie, sweetie. And I suppose I'll wish you goodnight too, Q."

"Call me tomorrow before you leave."

Sorcha groaned. "Don't remind me I'm leaving."

Quincy left with Evie, but not before giving Sorcha a kiss on the cheek. She wanted more, but she'd take whatever she could get.

She'd be on a plane home tomorrow night and had no plans to see Quincy before she left. *I guess sometimes you have to make your own magic.*

Fifteen minutes later, Linda's sister announced that the outdoor area was ready for everyone. Sorcha felt chagrined. She was supposed to help Laurel set up, but Laurel hadn't come to get her. *Oh well.* The DJ was playing music as they made their way outside.

The catering company had a large ATV with a makeshift bar on the back. They had tied streamers and small plastic sand shovels to the back bumper, in wedding-get-away-car fashion. Sorcha smiled to see the items dangling there.

She was standing in line to get a beverage when her cell phone rang. She snapped open her small clutch and grabbed her phone. It was Quincy. *He must be home and missing me already.*

"Hello?"

"I need you. Evie cut her foot. It's bleeding terribly. I'm taking her to the ER. Can you meet me there? I can't do this alone."

He needed her!

But she couldn't do hospitals.

She panicked.

"Quincy, I..."

"The hospital in Venice Gardens."

Not waiting for an answer, he hung up.

They'd just left! How did Evie cut her foot?

She imagined the blood. There was probably a lot of it if he was taking Evie to the hospital. Sorcha felt like she might faint. Looking around for a seat, she saw a bench on the patio. Plopping down, she took a deep breath.

She hadn't been in a hospital in years, not since her mom died. She couldn't. The couple of times she tried to go, she'd panicked before walking in.

The image of her mom lying on a hospital bed, desperate for a drink of water when the nurses had told them not to give her any flashed through her mind. She still felt the raw emotion of that immense grief ten years later.

She couldn't go.

Oh, Evie...

Chapter 27

"Are you all right?" Linda's voice pulled Sorcha out of her worry over Evie.

"No. I'm not."

"What's wrong?" Linda sat next to Sorcha and grabbed her hand.

"Evie's hurt."

"What happened?"

"I don't know. Quincy called and said she cut her foot. He's taking her to the hospital."

"Oh, no. Do you need to go?"

Sorcha looked at her friend and shook her head. "He asked me to, but I can't."

"You don't have to stay here for me. Go. You should go."

"No," Sorcha said. "I can't."

"Oh. The hospital."

Sorcha nodded as tears started down her cheeks. "I can't do it."

"Yes, you can. They need you. Quincy needs you."

Sorcha sobbed. She wanted to be there for Evie and for Quincy. But fear paralyzed her.

"Just a minute." Linda jumped up and rushed off. The satin fabric of her dress rustled as she moved.

Sorcha clasped her hands together to keep them from flailing about. Her stomach roiled, and she looked around for a garbage can.

Tiki torches lit the patio area. It wasn't dark yet; the sun was low on the horizon but still burned in its last hurrah before setting. Several of the wedding guests were milling about, taking off their shoes before heading towards the designated reception area on the beach.

Sorcha dipped her head. She didn't want any of the guests to see her tears. Here she was ruining her best friend's wedding. If she was a stronger person, she could have quietly exited and gone to the hospital; no one would have missed her unless Linda looked for her.

Linda rushed back, dragging Mason along by the hand.

"Sorcha, which hospital?"

"Huh? Oh, Venice Gardens."

Linda and Mason looked at each other. "That's not far. Ten minutes, maybe," Mason said.

"Right." Linda nodded, thinking. "I'll tell Mom and Laurel we'll be back as soon as we can."

"No!" Sorcha stood up, shaking her head. "You two are not leaving your wedding reception because of me."

"For you," Linda said. "Not because of you. You need to be there, and you need me to get you there."

"And I want to be with my wife. It's our wedding day," Mason said, grinning at Linda. "We'll get you there. We'll see what's happening and decide what's next."

As Sorcha shook her head no, Mason insisted. "I'm a nurse. Emergencies happen. We understand."

"No," Sorcha protested. "What's next is for you both to go down to the bonfire. Tell the DJ what you want to hear next and dance! I don't need a babysitter. I am the babysitter."

She thought about her minor role in Evie's life. Evie wouldn't miss Sorcha being there, but Quincy would. Quincy needed her. She might struggle to walk into the hospital, but she'd cross that roadblock when she got there. She looked at her phone. "I'll call for a ride."

"No." Mason reached out and put his hand on hers. "We've got the ride." He reached into his pocket and pulled out a set of keys. "Let's go."

Sorcha knew they'd rented a Mini Cooper convertible for the weekend. "There's not enough room for the three of us in that car."

"Sure, there is. Come on."

Mason led the way as Linda pulled Sorcha along with a couple of gentle tugs on her hand. *This can't be happening. I'm ruining their reception.*

Sorcha wanted to cry harder. At the moment she didn't know what was worse, Evie being hurt or the disruption to Linda and Mason's reception.

Sorcha could only imagine what they looked like to strangers as the car screeched to a stop in front of the Emergency Room door: a bride, a groom, and a bridesmaid in a tiny convertible. When the car came to a stop, Sorcha felt every muscle in her body freeze. She could not move.

Linda was holding her veil, which floated straight back three feet past the back bumper, with one hand as she twisted in the front passenger seat, trying to wrap an arm around Sorcha, who sat in the tiny back seat. Sorcha leaned forward, comforted by Linda's hand rubbing her exposed upper back in small circles.

Linda kept telling Sorcha that things were going to be OK, for Evie and for Sorcha. Mason chimed in with a few helpful facts about what to expect in the emergency room; he was a traveling nurse who'd worked in dozens of hospitals around the country. While there were differences, there were many standard protocols.

Sorcha was trying not to hyperventilate. To keep her mind off the hospital, she kept bringing her thoughts back to Evie's sweet face with its chubby cheeks, bright eyes, and sparkling smile.

"I can do this for her. I can do this for her." Sorcha kept this chant going in her head. Some of Linda and Mason's remarks made it through to her conscious thought, but concentrating on Evie kept her from panicking.

"You got this, Sor," Linda said, her hand reaching for Sorcha's.

"We'll be with you, Sorcha," Mason chimed in.

The gentle squeeze of Linda's hand finally snapped Sorcha out of her inaction. "OK."

In the waiting area, Sorcha's eyes scanned wildly. She could not see Quincy. Had they come to the right hospital?

Linda pulled her towards the receptionist's desk. "Hi. We're looking for—" A child's scream interrupted her words.

Sorcha twisted her head towards the sound. *Was that Evie?*

"So! So!"

That was definitely Evie calling for Sorcha.

"Those are my..." What? Friends? She wanted to say family.

"Oh! You're with the little girl," the man behind the counter said, leaning forward. "There, in the second bay. One of you can go back there, but not all three. Actually..." His eyes swept over each of them. "Shouldn't you be at a wedding somewhere?"

Sorcha turned and looked at Linda and Mason. They'd got her here, past the front door. She was in a hospital, and she hadn't freaked out.

She wanted to run towards the bay to get to Quincy and Evie, but she quickly hugged Linda and Mason. "Go. Go now. I'll be fine. I'll ride back with them. Go. Thank you for getting me here."

"Are you sure?" Linda asked, returning the hug. "You're OK?"

"Yes. I'm positive. Go."

Mason punched her lightly on the arm. "You got this."

Sorcha didn't watch them leave. She focused on stepping one foot in front of the other towards the door indicated by the receptionist.

Watching the floor and thinking about Evie helped her block the thoughts of the hospital itself. *It's a care center. She's getting the care she needs. We're going to be all right.*

Entering the room, she saw Quincy leaning over the bed, his head not far from Evie's. He slowly stroked the hair back from her face, repeating the movement over and over to calm her.

A nurse was holding gauze on Evie's foot. She was talking about preparing for stitches, and Sorcha started humming to herself to block the image of a needle out of her head.

Hearing the door, Quincy whipped his head around. "Sorcha's here!" he cried. "Look, Evie, it's So-So."

Sorcha took a deep breath and stepped to the opposite side of the bed. She kept her eyes locked on Evie, not daring to look at the machines and medical gear around the room. "Hi, Evie, sweetie. I'm here, baby girl."

Evie hiccupped and tried to smile. She glanced down at the nurse and cried, "Owww!"

Sorcha leaned down and gave her a kiss, wiping tears from the little girl's face with shaking hands. "What happened?" she asked, glancing up at Quincy.

"Some idiot broke a bottle in the sand and didn't clean it up."

"At The Mockingbird?" Sorcha's breath felt too quick and too shallow. *Breathe deeply. Calm down.*

"No, the beach near our house. Once we got home, I decided we'd take a stroll, get some fresh air before bed." He ran a hand over his head and rolled his shoulders. "We weren't out there five minutes before she stepped on the glass. It was..." He glanced at Evie. "Not good."

"What's happening now?" Sorcha glanced quickly at the nurse.

"She's going to get a few stitches once the bleeding slows."

The nurse chimed in, "Very soon."

Sorcha felt her face heat. *I'm not going to faint.*

"Are you OK?" Quincy's brow furrowed as he watched Sorcha.

"Don't worry about me." She waved her hand at Quincy and leaned closer to Evie. If she focused on Evie, she could ignore the machines and medical signs and the pain on Quincy's face. "Did you have fun at the wedding tonight? Everyone was talking about the pretty little girl in the fancy dress. You were as pretty as the bride."

If I keep talking, I don't have to think about where I am or what's happening here.

She didn't hear Quincy move, but she felt his hand on her back. "Hey," he said. "Are you sure you're all right?"

She took a deep breath and turned to him. "I'm fine."

If she said it enough, maybe it could be true.

He held her gaze, questioning. "Thank you for coming," he said, then he gave her a quick kiss before returning to the other side of the hospital bed.

Two hours later, they were finally out of the hospital.

Evie had fallen asleep before the paperwork was completed.

Quincy carried the sleeping child, and Sorcha followed them, eager to leave the hospital. The emotional toll of the last few hours equaled the physical toll of the busy week and long day celebrating her friends.

When Quincy got behind the wheel and started the car, Sorcha wanted to lean across the seat and rest her head on his shoulder.

"Am I taking you back to the reception?" he asked.

Sorcha looked at the clock. It was almost eleven. "Please. I'm not sure they will still be there, but I want to check. I can walk to the B&B from there."

She was tired, but she could rally for the reception. She must at least try to dance at Linda's wedding.

"Thank you for coming to the hospital. Evie calmed down once you arrived."

"That was calm?" Sorcha smiled.

"Comparatively. Again, thank you." Quincy's hand tightened on the wheel, and the veins on the back of his hand popped.

She wanted to say it was no big deal. Of course, she'd be there. But that wasn't true; it was a big deal. She was proud of herself and thankful to Linda and Mason for helping her find the courage to go. Another reason to get back to the reception; she needed to thank them.

"What time is your flight tomorrow?"

"Not until four. I can sleep in."

"That's good. Then what are your plans?"

"I'm meeting Linda and everyone for brunch and gift opening. I helped Laurel plan it."

Quincy was obviously trying to figure out if they could see each other before she left town, and Sorcha wanted to see them, but she felt hesitant.

Seeing Evie lying on that hospital bed had shaken Sorcha to the core. Walking into that room, she knew that the little girl's foot had been cut. It hadn't been life-threatening injury. It had been a quick fix; a few stitches, and they could go.

But seeing the medical equipment, the nurse and doctor examining Evie, had sent Sorcha back to the time when her mom was in the hospital.

That should have been okay, too. Surgery, maybe chemo, and her mom should have been home for Christmas. But it hadn't worked out that way.

There was so much danger and risk in this world. It was a miracle anyone made it to eighty.

How was she going to endure the stress of raising a child, who could run out into the street unexpectedly, who could get sick, who could make the wrong choice at any time?

She didn't know if she had the fortitude to be there for Evie and not fall apart if something else were to happen to her.

Quincy interrupted her thoughts. "So, we won't see you."

Sorcha shook her head. "I don't think so. Unless the luncheon ends early." She couldn't keep the doubt from her voice.

Soon Quincy pulled to the curb outside the Mockingbird. From her vantage point, she could see some of the wedding party still on the beach. The car windows were down, and she could hear the music, an Ed Sheeran song that she loved.

Every muscle in her body hurt like she'd worked out for eight hours today. She ached, she was cold, and she wanted to lie down.

She took a deep breath and turned to look at Evie, still sleeping in the back seat. She wanted to pull the child out of the car seat and hug her for hours. Then she looked at Quincy. She wanted to hug him for days. If this was going to be goodbye, why not make it a good one?

"I'd better go," she said. She unbuckled her seatbelt.

Quincy clasped her hand. He leaned forward and looked her in the eye. "Wait." He looked like he wanted to say something, but she threw her arms around him and kissed him before he could.

Quincy's hands moved to her head, holding her close as he shifted his head to deepen the kiss.

Sorcha tried to convey everything she wanted to say with the kiss. How she wished she was strong enough to stay. How much she cared for him and Evie. And just how easy it would be to fall in love with him, if only they had a bit more time.

She moved her hands to his face, her fingers in his beard. She pulled back from the kiss, knowing she had to leave before she started crying.

"Bye, Quincy. Give Evie a big kiss for me in the morning."

"I will. Since we won't see you tomorrow. Let me know when you get home safe."

She nodded and exited the car, just as the first tears began to flow.

Chapter 28

Sorcha fished two aspirins out of her purse. She'd stayed up so late with the wedding celebrants, talking and dancing until two in the morning.

She'd stumbled back to the B&B and collapsed, waking up late in the morning and hurriedly packing before Linda's sister picked her up for brunch.

Now she was sitting at the gate waiting for her flight to board. Besides the headache, she felt raw. She dreaded going home to the apartment, where she'd be reminded that Linda had moved out.

She still didn't have a clue what to do professionally. And now she realized whatever future she dreamed of with Quincy was a mirage.

Her phone rang. She wanted to ignore it. *Forty more minutes and I would have been in the air, anyway.*

The man sitting across from her leaned forward. "That one's you."

"Yeah, I know." *Shoot. So much for ignoring it.*

Pulling the phone out of her carry-on, she checked the caller ID. Quincy.

At least it will be a quick call. "Hey, Poppa Q."

"You haven't boarded yet," he said, foregoing a hello.

"Nope. Still waiting."

"Any chance you could come back to the main terminal? Evie has something for you."

"What? You're here at the airport?"

"Yes. Couldn't let you go without seeing you today."

"I'll be right there."

She hung up and grabbed her bag, checking the announcement board. Her flight would board in ten minutes. She hoped the security line wasn't too long, as she would have to exit and come back through.

She jogged down the terminal hallway past eight gates before getting to the exit doors. The pounding of her feet exacerbated the headache.

It was easy to find Quincy and Evie. The little girl was sitting on his shoulders, smiling and laughing at everyone from her vantage point.

"Hey, there." Sorcha put her hand on Evie's leg, looking at the bandage wrapped around the girl's foot.

Quincy leaned forward and kissed Sorcha on the cheek. "Hey, how much time do you have?"

"Not much. The flight will start boarding in a few minutes."

She noticed he held a small paper bag in one hand, even as he held onto Evie's legs.

"Here." He nodded towards the bag. "Take this."

He opened most of his fingers but kept a grip on Evie. Sorcha grabbed the bag and gave him a puzzled look. "This won't cause them to strip-search me when I go back through security, will it?"

Quincy laughed. "No. Open it now."

She opened the brown paper bag and saw two wrapped brownies, the decadent butterscotch ones she'd raved about when he'd bought them for her last week.

"Oh, the yummy brownies. Thank you!" She looked up at Evie. "Thank you, sweetie. You guys didn't need to drive all the way here to bring me goodies."

"Yes, we did. It's a thank-you for coming to our rescue last night."

Sorcha thought about Linda and Mason's support to get her into the hospital. "I didn't rescue anyone."

She'd needed rescuing just to show up for a hurt child.

"You were there for us when we needed you. That's a rescue. Thank you."

He wrapped a forearm over both of Evie's legs and pulled Sorcha to him in a side hug with his free arm. "Go. That flight doesn't want to leave without you."

What was she going home for? It felt like there was nothing there for her. But it was safe, known, comforting.

"Thanks, again."

She turned and walked to the security line.

If she didn't say goodbye, maybe it wouldn't hurt. Once she got past the identity check and dumped her bag onto the x-ray machine belt, she turned, assuming Quincy and Evie would be gone, but they stood where she'd left them. Evie was waving her arm, and Quincy was bouncing her on his shoulders. Sorcha could see his lips moving, but they were too far away to hear him. She waved and turned away.

Chapter 29

By Wednesday, Sorcha was so miserable that she called her stepmom Barb and asked if she could bring dinner over for the family. She wanted out of her lonely apartment and hoped that being around her family would get her out of her funk.

She exchanged a few cordial text messages with Quincy but didn't call him, hoping that not talking to him would help her get over him.

It didn't seem to be working.

Pulling into the family's driveway, Sorcha glanced at the house. It was the same house she'd grown up in. Sometimes when she came home, she would have a fleeting vision of her mom standing on the porch, waving, excited that she was home.

Not tonight.

Aiden jogged out of the garage towards her with a goofy grin on his face.

"Mom said to come help," he said as he got closer. "What'd you bring us?" Approaching her, he gave her a light punch on the shoulder.

"I brought you nothing," she responded. "The rest of the family gets pizza."

"Ah, man," he moaned, opening the passenger door. "Smells mighty fine."

"You can carry the boxes, and I'll get the door," Sorcha said.

They walked down the driveway and entered through the kitchen door. Aiden put the pizza boxes on the stove as Jacob came running down the stairs.

Her dad and Barb were sitting at the table, reviewing papers. Both stood up when she entered.

"Good to see you. Can't wait to hear about Linda's wedding," Barb said.

"Hi, honey," Dean said, embracing her in a tight hug. "Hey, after we eat, I'll take you for a drive through that new subdivision I told you about. We can look around, check out the houses."

Sorcha looked at Barb and tried not to roll her eyes. She must have been unsuccessful.

"Dean," Barb said sternly. "Drop it. You're applying too much pressure."

They sat down to eat and chatted about the wedding. Aiden and Jacob kept speaking over Sorcha, asking silly questions and interjecting childish jokes. As soon as they finished eating, Barb ordered Dean and the boys to go get dessert.

Jacob jumped up and rushed to the back door where their car keys hung from a small black hanger in the shape of a key. "I'm driving!"

"Dude!" Aiden whined.

"Pray for me," Dean said, standing and following the boys out the door.

"Now, let's head outside and get some fresh air," Barb said after the men had left.

"What about washing up?" Sorcha asked, indicating the glasses in the sink and the table that needed to be wiped off.

"The boys can do it when they get back."

Outside, they walked to the backyard where Dean had built a firepit and surrounded it with deep-cushioned chairs. It was one of the family's favorite places to relax in the evening.

"Now, tell me what's going on." Barb sat on the chair in the far corner and patted the one next to it.

Sorcha plopped down dramatically. "Everything feels wrong."

"That's broad. How about narrowing it down to one issue, to start with?"

Sorcha considered. Where to start? The job hunt, the Quincy question, missing sweet Evie, and missing her roommate. They were all important, and all seemed insurmountable.

"I'm not sure where to begin."

"That tone makes me think there is a problem of the male persuasion."

"Yeah." Sorcha smiled. "That's one of them."

"Who is this person? Tell me more."

"Quincy. He lives in Seaside Bay." She raised her eyebrows, as if to say 'See, it's a big issue.' Barb nodded, so Sorcha continued, "I met him last year when I went with Linda. He's incredibly sexy in a brooding motorcycle-club member way."

"He's in a motorcycle club?"

"No. He just looks like he is. Tattooed, bearded, wears all black. That sort of thing. Hold on. I have a picture on my phone." She showed Barb the photo of the three of them at Linda's wedding. "I look at this photo constantly."

"Hmm. Maybe not the sort of man you bring home to meet your dad."

"Right. But I would like to. Quincy looks rough, but he's not. It's just a shield he wears. He's always been respectful but aloof to me. Until recently."

"Not seeing the problem here, Sorcha."

"Well, for one, he lives in Florida. Two, he was just told he has a daughter, and now he has full custody of her. Long story. But he's great with her. And since I was there with nothing to do when he was in a jam, I helped him out by babysitting until he could find a permanent nanny."

"That was sweet of you."

"Sure. Seemed innocent enough, but I couldn't help falling in love with her. And with him, but I don't know how to move forward. It's so terrifying."

Barb looked alarmed and leaned forward. "What is?"

"Raising a child. They get hurt. I can't take it." Sorcha remembered walking into the hospital. She shuddered, thinking about the smell of antiseptic and blood. "His daughter stepped on glass in the sand and cut her foot Saturday night and had to go to the hospital. I froze. Linda and Mason left their own wedding to take me! You know I'm terrified of hospitals and I wouldn't have been able to walk in if they hadn't been there with me, encouraging me, holding my hand, talking to me about what to expect.

"What if I'd been home alone with Evie when she got hurt? How could I handle it? I completely froze when Quincy asked me to come to the hospital. Completely froze."

"You've had kids get hurt in your classroom before, right? On the playground? You've managed."

The birds that had scattered and quieted when they'd come outside returned to chirping and searching for bugs in the grass. Their noises, so natural and normal, were comforting. *This must be why Barb and Dad are so keen to spend time outside.*

"But there has always been someone else there to call. The school nurse. The principal. If I know there's backup, I'm okay. It's when I'm alone that I worry about."

"You'll find the strength to do it. When it's your kid, you do everything in your power to help them."

Sorcha knew Barb had managed lots of crises with her boys. They were athletic, hyper, and always roughhousing. The woman probably couldn't count on both hands how many times she'd rushed one or the other of them to prompt care or the ER. *There's been at least half a dozen since she's been married to Dad. Who knows how many more than that when the boys were younger?*

Sorcha nodded. Barb's words made sense. "But what if it's your stepkid? It's not the same, right?"

"Oh, Sorcha! Is that what you really think? That's wrong!" Barb threw her hands up and moved to sit on the arm of Sorcha's Adirondack chair. She leaned over and enveloped Sorcha in a hug. Sorcha put her hands on Barb's arms, enjoying the warmth and calm the embrace brought. "When you marry the man, you marry the family. His kids become your kids."

Sorcha wanted to argue. There's no way Barb felt the same way about her as she did about Aiden and Jacob. She couldn't. Yes, Barb could love Sorcha, though Sorcha hadn't given her a lot to love at first, she had felt all the normal angst over a stepparent when Barb and Dean married. But over time, she had accepted Barb as part of their family, and Barb must have accepted her, too.

"It's not always easy," Barb said. "You're learning how to dance with each other, as you learn in every new relationship. But you figure it out, how to parent when you're not their natural parent. How old is his daughter? And what's her name?"

"Evie. She's nineteen months."

"Oh." Barb patted Sorcha's arm and went back to her own chair. "She's young. Where's her mom?"

"She died."

Barb leaned forward and touched Sorcha's knee. Love filled her dark brown eyes. "You've got that in common. I think you'd make a fantastic stepmom, honey."

"I've got an outstanding role model."

They heard a car pull into the drive. "That must be the boys," Barb said. "Anything else you want to talk about alone? I can send them on another errand."

Sorcha smiled. "No, that helped. Thanks for listening and telling me that. I don't know where things will go from here, but it's good to hear your thoughts about being a stepmom."

Dean walked around the side of the house, holding a drink tray and large paper cups. "We're back."

"Goody. Dessert," Sorcha said, standing up.

"Yours is the one in front. Black raspberry. Barb's is the one by my left hand."

Sorcha grabbed the two shakes and offered the vanilla one to Barb.

"Should I start a fire?" Dean asked, sitting down.

"Where are the boys?" Barb asked.

"They wanted to walk home and stop by to see a friend."

"A friend, huh? What's her name?" Sorcha asked.

"We don't know," Dean said. "Aiden's not talking, but I think you're right; he's crushing on someone."

"Figures." Sorcha took a long sip of the shake.

"Hey," Dean said, tossing the drink holder on the cold firepit. "We drove by Linda's little store beside In Bloom. I think it's so creative. We saw it at a festival last month. It's great that she can drive it around wherever she wants to go. What was once a camper where people slept is now a store on wheels. Clever."

It was clever. Mason had bought the old Airstream for Linda, and Linda had made it her own. Sorcha had helped Linda decorate it with vintage and thrifted finds, and a few crafts they'd designed out of driftwood and shells.

Mason got a good deal on the trailer. A home away from home. A home that you could take wherever you wanted to go.

She wondered what Quincy would think about a home on wheels. He didn't require or want a lot of personal possessions. Of course, Evie needed things, too. Some larger families managed in a large recreational vehicle. Maybe that solved the location problem.

If only she could solve the employment problem and figure out where she stood with Quincy.

She was going to need another milkshake.

"Dad. Can we talk about the housing qualification part of my inheritance?"

Chapter 30

Sorcha made the last turn onto Quincy's street. She saw both his car and his motorcycle sitting on the curb in front of his house, so he and Evie were either at home, or taking a walk on the beach, one of their favorite things to do now that the cut on Evie's foot had healed.

Sorcha pulled to the curb and parked, turned off the engine of the pickup truck, and let out a slow breath. She'd taken a risk coming here unannounced. But when she shared her news with Quincy, she hoped it would pay off.

It was now mid-August and the Florida heat was almost suffocating when she jumped out of the truck.

Walking up to the front door, she thought about how July had passed in a blur. She'd spent most of her time filling out job applications, preparing for interviews, researching RVs, and having daily video calls with Quincy and Evie.

It was hard to keep the RV research from Quincy, but she didn't want to ruin the surprise.

In her downtime, she had pulled out her old sketchbook and tinted charcoal pencils and had attempted to draw the three of them at Linda's wedding. After countless sketches, she finally made one that she was proud of, which she'd hung above the dining table in the RV.

When they talked about the future, it was always hypothetical. Maybe they would end up in the same location.

Maybe Quincy would move to be closer to his sister. Or maybe Sorcha would move to be closer to Quincy. All 'maybes' with no definite decisions.

When Sorcha told Quincy she was nervous about a particular job interview coming up, he would send treats or call with a pep talk. His encouragement and kindness became the most reliable thing in her life.

In mid-July, Sorcha had taken a leap of faith and handed in her resignation at school. Several of the interviews had gone well, and she was confident the right job was going to land. On July twenty-ninth, it did.

It was a training coordinator role for a large telecommunications company. It was one hundred percent remote, the best part of the job. That and the nice salary. She was giving up the long summer break, but the ability to work anywhere outweighed everything she would miss about teaching. Except for the kids, she'd miss the classroom full of excited third graders.

With that offer in hand, she'd begun downsizing her wardrobe and other possessions. If she was going to be mobile like Quincy, she needed to lighten her load.

Now, standing on his doorstep, she wondered if he would think she was absolutely nuts.

She knocked twice and listened for any sounds coming from within. Soon, she heard Quincy's footsteps moving through the living room.

When he opened the door, she could hear children's music coming from the speaker on the side table. She glanced around and saw Evie playing on the floor with farm animals, a sheep in one hand, a cow in the other.

Evie turned towards the door when Quincy opened it. "So-So!" she cried, bounding to her feet and running.

Sorcha quickly glanced at Quincy again as she bent down to scoop up Evie. "Surprise," she said to Quincy, noticing the stunned expression on his face.

"What the what," Quincy said. He glanced outside and noticed the truck. "What's that?"

"Oh, I didn't mention my new truck?" she asked with a teasing lilt. She gave Evie a kiss on the cheek. "I've missed you so much, Evie-girl!"

"No," Quincy drawled. "Am I to assume that's your RV behind it as well?"

Sorcha beamed at him. "It is. Want to check it out?"

"I have dinner on the stove," he said, nodding towards the kitchen. "Can we check it out after we eat?"

"Of course! Let's get in and shut the door. It's too hot for tamales out here."

Sorcha followed Quincy into the kitchen, still carrying Evie, who was talking about cows and rain. Or at least that's what Sorcha thought she was talking about.

Quincy stirred something on the stove; it smelled like cheesy pasta. "We weren't expecting you. This must mean that when we chatted last night you weren't in your apartment."

"I wasn't," she said. "I was in a motel in Georgia."

Quincy chuckled. "I meant to ask about the wall color, but I kept getting distracted by your pretty smile."

"See, I have a hard time keeping a secret. My face is too expressive." She rocked Evie back and forth, noticing the child was slightly heavier than she'd been six weeks ago. Good.

"I think you have a few secrets to share."

"I do."

"Have you become a traveling teacher?"

"Nope."

"Tour guide?"

"Nope."

"RV driver for the circus?"

"Do those still exist? And no. You're not very good at guessing."

Evie fussed to be put down, so Sorcha obliged.

"Well, why don't you enlighten me after you give me a hug?" Quincy set the large spoon down, leaned against the counter, and opened his arms.

Sorcha quickly stepped into his embrace, relishing the feel of his arms around her. Six weeks without Quincy's hugs had left her aching for one; it felt like coming home. She knew at that moment that anywhere with Quincy would be home for her. Her address didn't matter. What mattered was being with him.

He squeezed her for a minute. He let out a long breath, and Sorcha smiled into his chest. *I think he missed me.*

"Want to sit down?"

"No, I've driven all day. It feels good to stand."

Quincy pulled back from the embrace and leaned down to kiss her. His lips were firm, his beard warm and soft. He was all the right contradictions. He pushed her hair back off her face to study her. "All right. I got my fill. Now spill."

Sorcha laughed. "You've been reading too many toddler rhyming books."

He shook his head, glancing at the pot on the stove, and Sorcha stepped back so he could stir it again.

She looked towards the living room to see Evie contentedly playing with her animals. "I have a new job," Sorcha began. "And it's fully remote. I can work wherever I want."

"And you want to work in the RV?"

"I do and I can. I'm outfitted with high-speed Internet, a large monitor and laptop hookup. Free to roam."

Quincy stood at the stove, his rigid back to her. "Did you stop by to say goodbye?"

"No. I missed you. And Evie. I thought I might hang out here for a while."

He turned towards her with a grin. "A while, huh?"

"Yes, I think you said your lease was up in September and then you might move on."

"I did say that." He turned to face her, a grin threatening to overtake his sour expression.

"So, maybe you wouldn't need to rent a moving van this time. The RV has some pretty roomy storage closets and drawers."

"Does it now?"

"It does. I sold and donated a lot of my things. I decided it was time to explore more and clean less."

"That sounds pretty amazing, but Evie and I can't just tag along with you while you explore. I can't find a job if we're moving every couple of days."

"We don't have to move every few days. We can stay for months, maybe even a year at a time."

"Oh, then I can work. Good. Sounds like you're open to hitching your wagon to mine. So to speak."

Sorcha laughed. "It's more like hitching yours to mine. We could possibly load your bike into the truck bed and one of us drive the car. I don't think we can hitch both of your vehicles to the truck and RV."

"You're right. I don't think that would work. Traveling logistics is one thing, but I want to be clear about our relationship. You're not just looking for a new roommate, or roommates." He glanced past her to Evie. "Are you?"

"No, Quincy. I'm not just looking for a roommate. I love you and Evie. I love the life we can make together. You're not always so forthcoming with your feelings, but I suspect you might feel the same way."

"Of course I love Evie," he said with a wicked grin, as he stepped towards her. "I'm a man of few words—"

"Tell me about it."

He wrapped her in his arms again. "Maybe if someone didn't run her mouth like a paid commentator on the news, I could get a few words in."

Sorcha raised her hand up and pretended to turn a key at her lips.

"As dead set as I've been against dating someone, you've managed to break me. In all the right ways. I didn't think I would ever fall in love again. I thought love wasn't for me, that I was broken and unlovable. But you looked past my rough exterior. You see something that I thought I'd lost. And I love you for that reason and a hundred more."

"Wow. For a man of few words, that was quite a speech. Could you repeat it? I think I heard the words 'I love you.'"

"Not repeating the whole thing. But I will say I love you again."

"And again?"

"Don't push your luck."

"All right. So, does this mean we're a couple? Officially?"

Quincy looked pained. "Labels scare me."

"Then no labels."

"But we're together. Exclusive."

It wasn't a question, but Sorcha affirmed anyway.

Quincy kissed her before letting her go. "I think the pasta is burning."

"Oh, no!" Sorcha put her fingertips on her lips when he turned his back to her. She wanted to fix the warm sensation in her memory. "Should I get Evie ready to eat?"

"Please. After dinner, I think we have some planning to do. You know," he said, turning towards her. "I could pack up Evie and me and be ready to roll in just a couple of hours."

Sorcha had known Quincy had tonight off. That was why she'd planned to arrive today.

"All right, Mr. Spontaneous." Sorcha laughed. "I think we need a little more planning than that. It's time to get out the map."

On Saturday evening, Sorcha took advantage of Ramona's scheduled shift and walked to Crabbie's to hang out with Quincy while he worked. She felt guilty for not watching Evie herself, but Quincy had said he didn't want to take any hours away from Ramona.

Earlier, they'd had a picnic on the beach and made some important decisions about their future. Excited about getting on the road and beginning their adventures together, Quincy would put in his notice at the bar and break his lease a month early. They would be on the road in two short weeks.

They'd agreed to travel until Evie was ready to start kindergarten. They didn't want to continue moving her around once she was in school.

Quincy told Sorcha that, while working, he wanted to go back to school and pursue a degree. She said she'd help him find some remote schooling options.

Walking into the bar, Sorcha thought the heat made the crowd a little more hyped-up than normal. She wondered if college kids were having a last fling before classes started. Maybe they were borrowing their grandparents' condos for the last summer hurrah.

Several men tried to buy Sorcha a drink, but she turned each one down. When one young man became rather persistent, Quincy stepped out from behind the bar to tell him to get lost.

"Sorry, my dude," the kid said, ready to risk his life and limbs.

"I'm no one's dude." Quincy seemed ready to punch the kid in the nose.

"I didn't mean to hit on your sister."

Sister? Do I look like Quincy's sister? I'm not sure how to take that?

Quincy stepped even closer, towering over the kid with the messy hair and starched polo shirt.

"She's not my sister. She's my girlfriend. Get lost," Quincy growled.

So much for no labels!

Sorcha stood up from her bar stool and kissed Quincy's cheek. "I could have run him off, you know."

"Part of my job is to bounce the dude bros." He shook his head. "I'm getting too old for this nonsense."

"No, you're not. And you're the best-looking man in this bar tonight."

"And you're the prettiest woman."

A familiar voice spoke behind Sorcha. "What am I, Quincy?" Sorcha recognized Winnie's voice.

Quincy rolled his eyes as Sorcha turned around to find Winnie and Rosalie standing behind her.

"Winnie! Rosalie!" Sorcha embraced each of them quickly. "I'm so glad you're here!"

"This is a surprise," Rosalie said. "Did you save us a seat?"

Quincy tapped the man sitting two stools away from Sorcha. "Sir, any chance I could get you to move down a seat? These incredibly sexy and smart women would like to sit together."

The man glanced at the women, smiled, and scooted over.

"Ladies," Sorcha said as they sat at the bar. "I've got the first round. I have lots of news to share!"

"Oooh, sugar, this is gonna be good!" Winnie said, sliding in next to Sorcha.

Sorcha glanced at Quincy. Yes, *it is. It's gonna be real good.*

Chapter 31

Epilogue...

Two months later...

Sorcha exited the RV with a plate of cut vegetables in her hand. Quincy had a small fire going and planned to grill the veggies for dinner.

Evie sat at the picnic table coloring with triangular toddler crayons.

After a long road trip to New Jersey to meet Quincy's mom, (they'd arrived in time to attend her retirement party), and to Illinois to meet Sorcha's family, they were now camped in Baton Rouge, Louisiana, for their first extended stay. Quincy had found a job managing a bar ten minutes away from the RV park, and Sorcha was settling into her new position nicely.

During dinner, they talked about several day trips they wanted to make to explore Louisiana. Sorcha had created a travel scrapbook, and they were diligent in tracking the memories of their life on the road.

They'd already learned so much about living and working together. Sharing ideas, working through disagreements, and finding acceptable solutions for both of them. And Evie.

Later that evening, after Quincy put Evie to bed, they sat next to the fire, enjoying a glass of wine. Neighbors were playing a hearty game of Euchre three RVs away, and they could hear the laughter and sounds of camaraderie drifting through the park. Somewhere a hound dog whined, and they heard a sharp, "Quiet, Frank!" before the dog stopped.

"Welcome to our new life on the road. Guess we'll need to learn to play Euchre," Quincy said, holding up his glass to clink.

"This is pretty cool."

Sorcha thought this life was spectacular. Quincy was a rock, a good balance to her wild energy and big ideas. And Evie was a sweet little girl who no longer called Sorcha "So-So". Now she was "Mama". It had startled Sorcha the first time she'd heard it. She thought it was her imagination, but she looked at Evie, whose face lit up with happiness. Looking at Sorcha, she repeated, "Mama", like it was completely natural.

Sorcha had to hide her tears until Evie busied herself with the stuffed orange cat Sorcha had made the toddler. She was hesitant to tell Quincy, but they'd vowed to be open and honest with each other, so she began to tell him just as Evie walked up and said it again.

Quincy's eyes had gone wide, and he'd looked at Sorcha quickly, as if to confirm his understanding. She'd shrugged and smiled. He'd pulled her into a tight embrace; the importance of the moment not lost on him.

Sorcha sighed and glanced up at the stars. Streetlights in this park were scarce, which bothered her at first, but now that they'd gotten to know their neighbors, she appreciated the ability to relax in the glow of a campfire, watching the stars.

Sorcha imagined all the sailors throughout history using the stars for navigation. As intriguing as that sounded, she appreciated being able to use an application to get where she was going and avoid the toll roads!

"I've been thinking," Quincy began.

"Uh, oh," Sorcha teased.

He leaned over and bumped her shoulder. "We said we'd find a permanent place to live when Evie starts kindergarten."

"Are you changing your mind about life on the road already?"

"No," Quincy laughed. "This is great for now."

"Good. I think so, too."

"I was just thinking about making our relationship status permanent."

"Permanently dating? I thought we already were."

"Oh, boy." He shook his head. "I'm terrible at this."

He stood up, and Sorcha worried he was going to walk away. Instead, Quincy kneeled in front of her.

"Sorcha, I never thought I would fall in love again. I had decided love, marriage, and babies were not for me. Then you and Evie came along and proved I know nothing about nothing. In a great way."

He reached out and clasped her hands. "Your enthusiasm, optimism, and joy are remarkable. You once said I was softer because of Evie. Yes, she's a part of it, but it's you, too. You saw something in me I'd forgotten about a long time ago."

Sorcha's eyes filled with tears. She wanted to kiss him but wouldn't interrupt him now.

"You reminded me it's OK to dream," he continued, "and to want things. Not to let your situation become fixed."

He paused and looked up at the night sky. "Being out here now under the stars with you reminds me of camping with my grandpa when I was a kid. No matter what else is going on, knowing that I'll find you here at the end of the day, I know I can make it through a rough day."

Sorcha murmured, "Same."

Quincy smiled. "Good. Because I have an important question to ask you."

"Yeah?"

"I know I'm not the easiest man to be around sometimes. But I'm working on being better. Better at listening, at compromise, and in expressing my feelings." He gave an exaggerated shudder that made Sorcha laugh. "Please know that I will always have your back. Our relationship will always be worth fighting for, and I'll do just that. Now, you don't have to give me an answer now. You can think about it." He reached into the front pocket of his jeans. "Sorcha, I will work hard every day of the rest of my life to make you happy. To be the man you want and need me to be. And it would be an absolute honor if you were to marry me when you're ready. No pressure to set a date. There's no pressure to even wear this ring if you don't want to. You can put it in a drawer somewhere. When you're ready, I'll be here."

He held out a ring, but it was hard for Sorcha to see through her tears. She leaned forward and threw her arms around him.

The impact caused Quincy to grunt. His body shook with laughter. "Was that an answer?"

Sorcha leaned back and smiled at him. "I didn't hear a question."

"No? Shoot. I screwed up the proposal." He shook his head. "Let me try this again. Sorcha Pedigo, will you marry me?"

"Yes, Quincy. I can't wait to be your wife."

He stood and lifted her in his arms. "Woo hoo!"

Quincy's shout must have woken Frank up, because the hound started howling.

Sorcha and Quincy looked at each other and yelled, "Quiet, Frank!" in unison.

Sorcha had never thought her life would look like this. This far exceeded her expectations. Under the stars with the man she loved, with Evie just a few feet away, was her favorite place in the world.

WHAT'S NEXT

Sorcha and Quincy's story continues in the fun bonus epilogue. See where they are several years later. Get it here

Thank you for reading *Beachside Bliss*! Please consider leaving an honest review on Amazon, Goodreads, Bookbub, or wherever you normally leave reviews.

Sorcha's best friend Linda is a minor character in my "In Bloom" series. If you haven't read the In Bloom series yet, you can get a free introductory novella to it, (visit my website at www.kasey-kennedy.com) where you will meet Anna Lee, Paige, Nica, Lauren, and Tilly. The In Bloom series is full of stories about finding yourself in this world, and finding someone you can fall madly in love with!

You can jump into the In Bloom series by checking out book 1, *Peonies for Paige,* on Amazon. She's dreaming of the big city. He just wants to settle down. They've planted love, but can they tend it long enough to reap forever?

ACKNOWLEDGEMENTS

First, I want to thank my husband, Tim, for supporting my writing dream. I love you!

A very heartfelt thank you to Teresa M, Jill H, and Paulette W for beta reading—thank you for your comments and attention to detail!

Thank you to the writing friends who encouraged me and held my feet to the fire: Lynn, Rebecca, Emily, Trish, Stephanie, Bryn, and so many others. I appreciate you and am always here to cheer you on!

Family is everything, and I want to thank my siblings, siblings-in-law, aunts, uncles, cousins, nieces, and nephews for all the encouragement. I love you infinity.

Thank you to the professionals who supported this project: Marisa F for Development Editing, Rebecca H for copyediting, and Stacy U for proofreading! Thank you for putting up with my crazy last-minute requests and ridiculous deadlines.

And a heartfelt thank you to you, dear reader, for taking a chance on this story.

ABOUT THE AUTHOR

Kasey Kennedy is an Illinois gal through and through. She grew up in Central Illinois, finished college at Southern Illinois University Carbondale, and, soon afterward, moved to Chicago. She's been in Chicago or the surrounding suburbs ever since.

Kasey is happily married to her husband Tim and loves spending time with him—especially when that involves live music! If not attending a live show, they are usually listening to music, visiting family, watching movies, or planning their next trip.

When not dreaming up new characters and stories, Kasey is reading or planning what to read next. Occasionally, she pulls out the guitar that she has been trying to learn for 30+ years and strums enough to annoy her cat, Pepper.

Keep in touch. You can find me at:

f   facebook.com/KaseyKennedy8

◉   instagram.com/KaseyKennedy8

BB bookbub.com/authors/kasey-kennedy

g   goodreads.com/author/show/22679403.kasey_kennedy

a   amazon.com/author/kaseykennedy8

Visit my website to sign up for my newsletter. Your email address will never be shared and you can unsubscribe any time you wish.
www.kasey-kennedy.com
I love hearing from readers! You can email me at kasey@kasey-kennedy.com

www.ingramcontent.com/pod-product-compliance
Lightning Source LLC
LaVergne TN
LVHW040047080526
838202LV00045B/3535